The Magic

Lisa lives in the mountains
two ponies, two dogs, two c
was twenty months old, she
to travel across Europe. One day,
the M25, she began to think, 'Wouldn't it be good if the
campervan could fly?' So began the idea of The Magic
Campervan books.

In the adult world, she teaches online fiction and non-
fiction courses for the universities of Oxford and York, as
well as doing workshops and writing retreats in the
Algarve. She is the author of *The Trials of Tricia Blake*
(YA fiction), *A Divine War* (YA fiction), *The Last Dance
over the Berlin Wall* (fiction), *The Strange Tale of
Comrade Rublov* (fiction), *Beyond the Sea – Stories from
the Algarve* (fiction) and *Writing Fiction Workbook* (non-
fiction). She has also edited a collection of writings from
seventeen authors inspired by the Algarve, entitled *Summer
Times in the Algarve*.

For more information visit www.lisaselvidge.net or contact
her at lisa.selvidge@sapo.pt

THE MAGIC CAMPERVAN

BOOK 1

The Forbidden Slide

To Uncle Keith,
Nick, Fiona +
Saffron
With love
Tessa xx

The Magic Campervan, Book 1, The Forbidden Slide

Published by **Montanha Books**

Typeset in point 13 Times New Roman

ISBN: 978-989-53400-0-2

Cover image and illustrations by Paula Watt
Cover design by Cherry Anne Puddicombe

The Forbidden Slide

Portugal, United Kingdom (Norwich, Skegness, York, Glasgow), Iceland) and the Faroe Islands (Tórshavn)

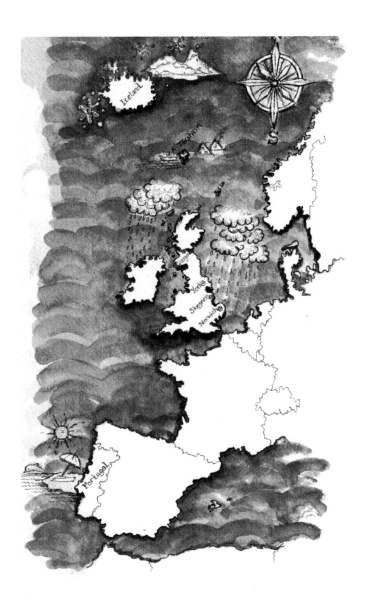

For Leo

Chapter 1 – The Strange Girl

Zoe's legs pounded up the staggered steps to the slide in their park in Norwich. Her teacher, Miss Colman, had told them in class earlier that Norwich was 'a fine old city'. Fine or not, Zoe thought the spelling was definitely not fine. Why wasn't it Norridge, like porridge? Or even Norage, like forage?

'English spelling is old and no longer phonetic,' Miss Colman had explained. 'That means it is not written as it sounds. Unlike Spanish or Portuguese, for example.'

That might well be true. Zoe had been to Alicante in Spain and had read quite easily 'ae-ro-puer-to' (airport) and 'es-pi-na-ca' (spinach – which should, of course, be 'spinidge', Zoe thought – if the horrible stuff really must exist). True, but it didn't help as they had to learn English. But the slide was fine and not at all old. It was one of those wide silver ones that rolled down the hill in waves.

'Come on, Vincent,' Zoe shouted behind her. 'They'll be here soon!'

They needed to go on before the big boys arrived. And horrible Sheena who sat behind her at school and stuck her chewed out chewing gum in her hair. For now, Zoe and her neighbour, Vincent, had the slide to themselves. Almost. A girl, with two long blonde plaits, appeared at the top before them. She must have run up the slide. That wasn't allowed.

'Hey!' Zoe called out. But the girl disappeared as quickly as she appeared.

Whoosh!

Wow!

She flew down.

Zoe watched, open-mouthed, from the top. Behind the girl the slide shone gold like rays of sunshine.

'Vincent! Did you see that?'

'It's because it was wet,' Vincent explained. Vincent always had an explanation.

The strange girl smiled up at them from the bottom. The shiny golden surface faded as she skipped away in just her socks, as if a cloud passed over the sun.

'Quick, Vincent. Before she comes back.' Zoe pushed Vincent down the slide but he hardly seemed to move, let alone leave a golden streak behind him.

'It's rubbish,' Vincent called up. 'It's too dry now.' He ran off to play in the sandpit.

Before she knew what was happening, Zoe had a naughty moment. Her mother would be furious but she pulled off her black school shoes and clattered them down the metal slide. Her big toe poked through her white-mucky beige socks. Then she pushed herself down the slide. And stopped. With shoes, or without, made no difference. Vincent was right: it was rubbish. Her bottom felt as if it was glued to the slide. She got off and scowled at the sky-grey metal. Perhaps if she took off her skirt?

A distant voice said, 'Zoe, can you come and put your coat on please. It's cold and it might rain.'

Zoe pretended not to hear her mother but maybe taking off her skirt wasn't a good idea. The girl was at the top again. Zoe watched her fly down as if she was sliding on water. Behind her the slide shimmered sky blue. BLUE? The girl turned to go up again. The blue faded back to grey.

Zoe slipped her shoes on, flattening the backs. She ran up behind the girl and pushed in front. 'Hey, it's my go!' she said, panting.

The girl smiled and stepped out of the way. Zoe pushed past and sat down where the girl had gone but, again, it was like pushing her way through the playdoh her mother used to make. Behind her the slide was as grey as the flat Norfolk sky above her.

'Zoe!' Her mother again.

Zoe got up and watched the girl fly down, her blonde plaits flapping behind her like Dorothy in *Wizard of Oz*.

Whoosh!

This time the slide shone PURPLE.

Zoe stood rooted to the spot as the girl bounced up and headed to the slide again. It was not possible. How would Vincent explain that? Zoe ran after her. When she got to the top she had another naughty moment. She pinched her arm. Hard. The girl yelped and looked at her. She was taller than Zoe, probably older, maybe ten.

'Why did you do that?' she asked calmly.

'Do what?' Zoe said. 'You are real then?'

'Of course I'm real. My name is Lilly.' She looked at her arm. 'It doesn't matter.'

What did she mean it didn't matter? Sheena would have not only pulled her hair but stamped on her toes and thrown her down the slide. Zoe pinched her again.

'That's not nice. But it's okay,' Lilly said. 'I used to do that.'

'What?' Zoe felt confused. What did she mean? 'This slide is rubbish. I know where the fastest slide in the world is!' she boasted. 'We're going there one day. Like tomorrow.' She didn't like the girl's smile. Silly Lilly.

'That's great,' Lilly said, before flying down the slide.

Zoe shuffled down the grey metal. She didn't want to go up again. She spat on it. Like Sheena did. A big glob of spit hit the metal and stuck there before snailing down. Zoe

looked over at her mother who was talking to another mum, probably Silly Lilly's. Then looked down. Lilly's sunbright yellow shoes were in the sand near the bottom of the slide. Then Zoe had one of her naughtiest moments yet. She scanned the park. Lilly had disappeared again. No one was watching her, except a little bird who was pecking at what looked like a piece of chewing gum in the sand. Zoe kneeled down and dug like a dog with a bone and did the most terrible thing: she buried the shoes in the sand. A smile of satisfaction crept across her face.

She skipped over to get Vincent from the sandpit and raced him to the swings. She was two years older than Vincent and at least a book taller, an encyclopaedia-size book. She won.

The other mother called for Lilly. Silly Lilly looked for her shoes but she couldn't find them. Lilly's mother came over. She smiled at them.

'Hello! Have you seen Lilly's shoes?' she asked.

Zoe shook her head, darting her eyes to the side to check that Vincent was doing the same.

'She wasn't wearing them on the slide,' Zoe said.

'I left them here,' Lilly said, staring at the spot where the shoes had been.

To Zoe's surprise, Lilly's mother didn't start shouting at Lilly for losing her shoes. Instead, she crouched down and Lilly climbed on her back. Then she smiled at them.

'Nice to meet you, Zoe and Vincent,' the mother said. 'If you find them, let us know!'

As they left the park they turned and waved. They were still smiling. Even shoeless. Zoe looked down and pushed Vincent on the swing. He wobbled from side to side.

'Zoe! Will you please put your coat on,' her mother shouted, coming over to her, carrying her navy-blue boring coat. She had wanted a purple one but her mother had said it was too expensive and against school regulations. 'And put your shoes on properly.'

'What? They are on.' She pushed the coat away. 'I'm not cold.'

'It's about five degrees, Zoe. It is cold.'

Zoe ran to the see-saw. Vincent ran after her.

Her mother flapped her coat, huffing and puffing like the big bad wolf. Zoe knew she was about to lose a star. Or worse. But, really, how had that girl slid down the slide so FAST? And why had the slide turned GOLD, BLUE and PURPLE? And why hadn't she pinched her back? She was definitely not from Norwich. She must be an extra-terrestrial.

Her mother paced around her.

'Okay, we're going,' she said. 'Vincent, come here.'

Zoe ignored her and sat down on the see-saw so Vincent couldn't get off.

'I can't, Lizzie,' Vincent said.

Sure enough, her mother started shouting at her and told her she'd lost a star. Zoe slowly let Vincent off and together they walked with her mother out of the park. Just in time as Sheena and about six of her friends were coming down the road. Sheena was allowed out on her own. Zoe's mother wouldn't let her.

Zoe put her head down and thought about the sunshine yellow shoes beneath the dirty sand. She wanted to go and get them but knew that she would lose a million gazillion stars if anyone found out what she'd done.

'I don't understand why you can't do as you're told, Zoe?' her mother was saying.

Zoe didn't know either. It wasn't that she didn't want to be good. It was just that she always seemed to do the

14

opposite. And the more her mother got cross, the more she did what she wasn't supposed to. And the crosser her mother got until they were all crossed up. She kicked the pavement with the tips of her black scraped shoes.

'Don't do that, Zoe. You'll ruin your shoes. And we can't afford any more.'

Zoe scuffed them again.

'Zoe!' her mother screamed. 'What did I just say?'

'I don't know,' said Zoe.

'I need a holiday!' her mother said. 'The mother I was talking to, Claudia, I think her name was, and her daughter have just driven back from Portugal in a campervan. Spent a month there. Had a fantastic time. Even in April. Wouldn't it be great to have a campervan.'

'What's Portugal?' Vincent asked.

'It's phonetic,' Zoe said, remembering what Miss Colman had said. 'Much easier than English.'

Both Vincent and her mother frowned at her.

'Portugal is a country, like England, but much hotter,' her mother explained.

'How much hotter?' asked Vincent.

'About twenty degrees,' said her mother.

That sounded hot, too hot. 'I don't like hot countries,' said Zoe.

'Me too,' said Vincent.

'Well that's fortunate,' her mother said. 'Because we're not going to Portugal and it's not hot here.'

'Mummy, where is the fastest slide?'

'*I* don't know.'

'Can we go?'

'Of course not.'

They walked between the cars and the houses, grey cardboard shoeboxes her mother called them. There were no shops, unfortunately, between the park and their house, but Zoe had a feeling that there would be no sweets or treats today anyway. She kicked a pizza box. Tut-tut-tut, her mother tutted. They passed a garage. Outside was a strange vehicle. A shiny silver campervan, higher than a mini-bus and with two big boxes on top, one slightly higher than the other. It had a window at the side and a nose like a dolphin. Zoe thought it winked at her but, of course, it didn't. Someone must be inside pulling down a shutter.

'Come on,' said her mother, stopping at the curb. 'Let's cross the road.'

'Wait!' said a man in a dirty white shirt and old faded jeans, rushing round the front of the camper towards them. 'This is for you, I reckon.'

The man held out a shiny key to Zoe's mother. Lizzie stopped and smiled, holding Zoe and Vincent back.

Vincent broke free, ran up to the man and took it.

'Vincent!'

'Vincent?' the man said nodding, looking first at Vincent, then Zoe, then her mother. 'They said to give it to a woman with red hair, Lizzie, and two children, Zoe and Vincent. That's you, I reckon. It's the key for the campervan.'

Chapter 2 – The Mystery Campervan

'What do you mean?' Lizzie said. 'Give it back, Vincent.'

Vincent studied the key carefully. Zoe snatched it from him. Vincent was useless at reading. On the key ring were two letters, M and E. ME. 'Me,' said Zoe.

'I know that,' said Vincent, snatching it back. 'Me!'

'Don't snatch, Vincent.'

'Vincent, give the key back to the man please.'

'No, really,' the man insisted. 'The campervan is for you. They were absolutely sure. You remember the woman you were talking to in the park? Claudia? Had a little girl. Rose or Tulip? Lost her shoes.'

'Lilly,' Zoe spat out, as if she were eating spinach.

'Ah yes. Lilly. Lovely girl. Lovely Mum too. Well, they've left it for you. They told me to give you the key. They said you needed to go somewhere. Why anyone would do that I don't know. Fine people. The documents are in the glove compartment. I think you'll find they are in your name. I've checked her over, changed the oil and put new tyres on. Can't do much more than that as the chassis is all closed. Never seen one like it. Must be a Portuguese make. But she's a beaut.'

Vincent pressed a button on the key and a side door swished open.

'Wow! Come on! What are we waiting for?' Zoe cried. 'Come on, Mummy!'

Lizzie was standing, her mouth opening and closing, as if she was trying to form words but couldn't. 'B... Wha... Ho... Wh...?'

'Go!' the man said. 'This could be the biggest adventure of your life. And the greatest journey. I guess you just bring it back here when you're done. They said they would be in touch. I think this is your golden ticket.'

'Hooray! Are we going to a chocolate factory?' Vincent asked.

'Somewhere much better, I'm sure,' the man said. He smiled and walked away leaving Lizzie staring after him, her mouth hanging open. Zoe followed Vincent inside. Wow! Inside it was more like a bus than a mini bus. It was huge. GIGANTIC. Bigger than their HOUSE. To the right were the front seats, and behind them there were three more seats (or a sofa) and a table. Further along there was a kitchen with lots of cupboards. At the back was a small bed and next to that a door. Zoe rushed to open it. A toilet and a shower! And a wardrobe! And cupboards with pots and pans, cups and glasses, kettles and juicers. A video screen in the back of the driver's seat. Everything. It had everything. On the ceiling there was another bed that came down. And a thick, soft purple carpet on the floor. Purple was her favourite colour.

'It's got a fridge!' Vincent screeched. 'And, look, here's chocolate!' His brown eyes gleamed as he distributed three bars of chocolate. Vincent ripped open the orange one, which Zoe saw said 'laranja'. He gave the red one to Zoe.

'Mummy! Come on, Mummy!' said Zoe, noticing she was still standing outside on the pavement. 'Are you catching flies?'

'My goodness, Zoe. I'm not sure about this. Why would someone give us a campervan? It doesn't make sense. It must cost a fortune.'

'Here, Lizzie, have some chocolate,' Vincent said handing her the green bar.

'No, Vincent, put it back.'

18

'But, Mummy, you said you wanted a campervan,' Zoe said. Was she never happy? Zoe crammed the chocolate into her mouth, trying not to think of Lilly's shoes.

'Yes, but… what if we get a big bill afterwards? I mean nothing is free in this world.'

'Mummy, the man said it was for us.'

'De ye tink it talks?' Vincent asked, his mouth full of chocolate.

'Of course it doesn't talk,' Lizzie replied. 'And neither should you with your mouth full. You shouldn't have eaten that. It's not ours.'

Vincent swallowed. 'There's a computer.' He pushed his way through to the front seats.

'That's a GPS,' Lizzie explained. 'That will tell us which way to go. Oh dear, it's a left-hand drive. And look at all those buttons. Okay, first things first, kids. We're going to go home and think what to do.'

Zoe and Vincent protested with moans and groans, whines and sighs.

'We need to find the best slide,' Zoe declared.

'Or a chocolate factory,' said Vincent.

'No,' Lizzie said firmly. 'We need to go home and talk to your mum, Vincent, to see if she can come on a little trip with us. If she can't then I'm not promising. I don't think I can do it on my own. It's the weekend but you can't just take time from school. You've only just started back after Easter. I'll be fined. We have to plan this. And if we do go I need one hundred per cent cooperation. Any whining will mean we are not going anywhere. Is that understood?'

She wasn't saying 'no'. Zoe pretended to frown but nudged Vincent to stop him from ruining their chances.

'Okay, Mummy.'

'Okay, Lizzie.'

19

'Right, let's get you two belted up. There are two booster seats. That's useful.'

Zoe was about to say that she didn't need the seat but she swallowed her words, jumped on the seat next to the window and pulled down the seatbelt. Vincent scrambled next to her. Her mother slotted the seatbelt into place with a 'Bing'.

'Right, can I have the key please, Vincent?'

Vincent reluctantly let go of the key.

'A strange looking key,' Lizzie commented, going to the driver's seat. 'Right, now, what do I do? There's no ignition.'

'You just press that button,' Vincent said.

How Vincent knew, Zoe didn't know, but it did say 'Start/Stop'.

Lizzie pressed the button. Lights flashed on the dashboard but no engine.

'You need to put your foot on the break,' Vincent explained.

'Vincent, you are only seven. How do you know?'

'Because of my racing games.'

Lizzie shook her head but did as Vincent said. The engine rumbled into life. A low powerful purr like a cat that has been stroked forever.

'Put on the computer and see if it talks,' Vincent said.

'No, Vincent, I think we know the way home. And, of course, it doesn't talk. It's a van. Real vans don't talk.'

Lizzie fastened her seatbelt and adjusted the mirror.

'Oh dear, I've never driven anything so big.'

'Are we going to crash?' Vincent asked.

'I hope not,' Lizzie said, pulling out onto the Ring Road. 'Wow. It almost seems to drive by itself.'

Zoe sat grinning. This was sooo exciting. She remembered the golden-blue-purple slide behind Lilly. The kind look in her eyes when she pinched her. What kind of child was she? Someone who didn't hit her when Zoe hurt her. Even smiled.

The campervan purred as it took them past the off-licence, the pizza take-away, The Rose pub. They turned onto City Road, right down Hospital Lane and left onto Hall Lane. Zoe waved to people walking along the pavement but no one seemed to be looking. Or maybe they couldn't see in. Only the green leaves on the trees waved back to her.

'Phew,' Lizzie breathed, pulling up just outside their houses. 'Okay, let's go and talk to your mum, Vincent.'

Zoe and Vincent pinged open their seatbelts and leapt out of their seats. The door swished open.

'Mummy, Mummy!' Vincent yelled.

'Annie!' Zoe ran after him.

Annie was at home between jobs working as an admin something at the university and at the pub. Lizzie went up to speak to her. Annie lifted up her glasses and wiped her eyes as she listened. Zoe waited to hear the verdict. She grabbed Vincent's hand and held on tightly.

'So it would be for three or four days. The kids can take a couple of days off school,' Lizzie explained. 'We can say they were sick. And I don't work until Wednesday. But I would really like you to come.'

'I can't, Lizzie, I'm sorry. I'm working and Vincent's dad is coming soon to take Vincent for the weekend.'

'O-oh,' groaned Zoe.

'Oh please, Mummy,' Vincent whined.

Annie's phone started chirping. Annie swiped it. 'Hello Tom.' She turned and walked into the kitchen.

Zoe looked at her mother.

'No whining,' she said. 'Even if Vincent can come, Annie can't, and I don't think I can do this on my own.'

Zoe noted the 'don't think'. She sighed. Loudly. Annie's muffled shouts seeped out of the kitchen. Zoe could only make out one sentence, 'It's always the same with you! Why…'

Zoe didn't see why grown-ups were allowed to whine and they weren't. If they had a star system they would never have any stars. Except perhaps for Lilly's mum. Zoe decided she was going to give stars for her mother. At the moment she had minus zero. The kitchen door slammed open and Annie marched in.

'Okay, Tom can't come this weekend. Something's come up with his work. He said to say sorry, Vincent.'

'Hooray!' Vincent said. 'So can I go with Zoe?'

'Can you manage?' Annie asked Lizzie. 'I'm really sorry. I have three sessions at the pub this weekend. I'll help you pack up and make them some spaghetti.'

Lizzie sighed deeply and ran her fingers through her shoulder length red hair so that the ends poked out between her fingers. Zoe looked into her mother's green eyes. Zoe had dark eyes and long black hair. People often said she must take after her father but Zoe didn't have a father. Her mother had wanted her so much that she had gone to the doctor's and they had made her without a father. Zoe didn't mind that. She couldn't imagine what it would be like to have two parents telling her what to do. That must be awful. But, even though her mother said that she was the most important person in the universe to her, sometimes, Zoe thought, she seemed to forget that. There were so many things that seemed to come before her. For example:

Work.
A cup of tea in the morning.
Cleaning the house.
Tidying up.
Cooking dinner.
Shopping.
Lying down for half an hour.
Glass of wine with Annie.
Facebook.

But now she had a chance to earn a star. *Please, Mummy.*

Lizzie looked at her. Then Vincent.

Chapter 3 – 'M'

'Yippee!' screamed Zoe and Vincent excitedly. 'We're going on holiday in a campervan! We're going to find the fastest slide in the world!'

'Well, we'll see about that,' her mother said. 'Go and pack a bag full of clothes and any toys you want to take,' Lizzie said. 'Don't forget your toothbrushes. And Vincent, don't forget your comb. Annie has told me how you never comb your hair. Then go to Vincent's for tea. We will leave in an hour. Might as well make the most of the weekend.'

'But where are we going, Mummy? Where is the fastest slide?'

'I will have a look online,' Lizzie said. 'But it is still only April. Many campsites might be closed.'

Zoe rushed out of the door and into her house. She must not forget Milly Monkey and Chipeto the donkey. They would both want to go on the fastest slide in the world with her. And her red blanket.

In just over an hour they were all piling into the campervan. Lizzie was taking deep breaths.

'Okay, the biggest slide heading north is in York which would take about five hours. I don't know if it's the fastest but I would guess if it's the biggest it would be the fastest. So we'll do two hours now, stop at a campsite and then head off again tomorrow morning. We will stay at a campsite in York for two nights. Then come back home. Okay?'

'Hooray!' yelled Zoe. 'Thank you, Mummy.' She went over and kissed her all the way up her arm. Her mother would definitely get a star for this. If not eleven.

Vincent headed straight for the GPS and switched it on. A map appeared.

'Vincent, what are you doing?'

'Just seeing if it...'

'Vincent, leave it alone please. I've already programmed it. Right, do we have iPad, DVD, books, crayons?' Lizzie went around checking all the cupboards. 'We have soup, bread, pasta, beans, sauces, biscuits, eggs, bananas, Marmite and lots of milk and water.'

'What's that there?' Vincent said, about to push a button with 'M' on it.

'Vincent, if you want to come with us, SIT DOWN.'

'But I just want…'

'Vincent.'

'All right.' Vincent sat down and they binged up.

'Are we ready?'

'Yes!' Zoe cried.

The engine rumbled to life. Lizzie put the van into 'D' and drove off but even before a few minutes had passed they were stuck in a traffic jam on the ring road.

'Oh dear, it's rush hour traffic on a Friday evening.'

They crawled and crawled, inching forward. The grey sky became greyer.

'A snail would be quicker,' Zoe said.

'Or an aeroplane,' added Vincent.

'Indeed.'

They rolled forward a few more metres.

'Are we nearly there yet?' Zoe asked.

'No. I'm going to stop at the petrol station,' Lizzie said. 'Would you like anything?'

'Ice-cream! Ice-cream!'

As soon as her mother climbed out the camper, Vincent released himself and went straight to the computerised dashboard.

'Vincent! Mummy won't like that!' Zoe said.

'I just want to…' He pressed the 'M'. A green light came on.

Zoe thought she heard someone clearing her voice – as if about to speak.

H-ke. H-ke.

She looked around, confused. Just then, her mother climbed back up to get her purse. It must have been her.

'Vincent! What are you doing? Sit back down please. Oh goodness, what's that green light?' She pressed it and off it went. 'Did you switch that on? Okay, no ice-creams.'

'Oh please, Mummy. *I* didn't touch it,' Zoe said. She hit Vincent.

'Oh dear,' her mother said. 'I'm going to have a coffee. I'm tired. We shouldn't have come.' She walked away.

Vincent pushed out tears. Zoe ignored him. Something felt wrong but she didn't know what. This time she got out of her chair and pressed the green light. The half-cough again.

H-ke. H-ke.

'H-ello,' said a voice from the speakers in the camper.

'Hello?' called Vincent. His tears disappeared back into his eyes. 'Where are you?'

'I'm here, Vincent, thank you. You knew. And, hello Zoe.'

Zoe looked in astonishment at Vincent.

'My name is Efemérida but call me Merida. Nice to meet you.'

'Wow! You really talk,' said Zoe, her mouth slightly open.

26

'But I knew that. I lost my ice-cream,' Vincent said. 'That's not fair.'

'You must forgive Lizzie, Vincent. She's doing her best. Here she comes. Zoe, you'd better sit down.'

Zoe scrambled back into her seat, amazed. A talking campervan. Her mother climbed into the van and gave Zoe and Vincent a Cornetto each.

'There you go. I'm sorry...'

'That's good that you say, 'sorry', Lizzie,' Merida said. 'Hello, by the way, I'm Meri....'

'What the merry...!' Lizzie bolted upright and spun round.

'That's what I was trying to show you,' Vincent pointed to the green light.

Lizzie stared at it. She put out her arm to switch it off.

'Please don't, Lizz...'

Lizzie pressed it.

'Mummy!'

Merida disappeared. Zoe would take a star off for that.

Lizzie sat in the driver's seat, fastened her seat belt and switched on the GPS. 'Turn left onto the Ring Road.'

'One computer talking is enough,' she said. 'I need to concentrate.'

Zoe and Vincent exchanged knowing looks as they tore off the ice-cream wrappers.

'Merida's not a computer,' Vincent said quietly.

'Merida? Oh dear.' Lizzie snorted. 'Of course it's a computer,' she said, driving off. 'Like Siri, I suppose. Sirida. Right, off we go again. See how far we get this time!'

Not far. In less than five minutes they were bumper to bumper again. Big fat black and silver cars, and even bigger trucks and lorries, blocked the roads. The grey sky enveloped them all. Only the green trees lining the road waved to them. Zoe and Vincent ate their ice-creams. Vincent got his all over his curly hair. Zoe suspected that Merida might be able to help them but grown-ups are so disbelieving, her mother in particular. It was almost unbelievable how unbelieving she could be. Once Zoe had picked some flowers, put a ribbon around them and left them on the kitchen table. Her mother had called around all her friends first before she'd believed that they were from Zoe. And once, when she was still only five, her mother had refused to believe that she had found her way home on her own after her mother had lost her in Jarrolds. And she never believed her when she told her all the horrible things Sheena had done to her. Neither would her mother believe her when she felt ill and didn't want to go to school. She was horrible then.

Vincent opened his iPad, resting it on the table in front of them, and they played a pancake app, mixing up the egg, flour, butter and milk, frying them, tossing them up and then adding different toppings. They ignored her mother's sighs and sudden exclamations.

'Look Zoe! This is a strawberry jam-chocolatey-mint-honey-and cheese one! Yummy!' said Vincent.

They tapped their fingers to eat the pancakes.

It started raining.

'Ah!' said Lizzie as the wipers started automatically and the headlights came on.

'At the next roundabout take the second exit,' said the GPS.

Lizzie pushed their way round together with the other cars and lorries. 'Oh my goodness.'

'What Lizzie?' Vincent said.

'We will never get there,' Lizzie said, turning round. 'Oh, look at your hair, Vincent. It's covered in ice-cream.'

'Why don't you switch on Merida?' Vincent swiped at his dark curls with the back of his hand. 'She will help us.'

'Right,' she said, and pressed the green button. 'Let's ask a campervan for help, shall we. What a good idea,' Lizzie's crossness spilling out into her voice. 'Hello Merida? The children seem to think you can help us. We are stuck in traffic. I've told them it's just a load of gobbledygook but they insist.'

'H-ke. Hello, Lizzie. Thank you for switching me on again.'

Lizzie fell silent. 'Who are you? What are you? Are you like Siri?'

'Siri! Not at all. People call me Efemérida or simply Merida. It's a Portuguese word. And Spanish. It means Mayfly. I don't mind which you call me.'

'But that's not possible,' Lizzie said.

'Why not, Lizzie?'

'Because technology is not that advanced.'

'I was made by a very special person.'

Lizzie shook her head as if to shake her ears to get rid of the voice.

'Merida?' Vincent called. 'Can you help us please?'

'Of course I can, Vincent. What do you want me to do?'

'We want you to take us to the biggest, no, the fastest, slide in the world!' Zoe cut in.

'Ah yes. Well, I see you're already programmed to go to York where there is a big Astra slide. But not, strictly speaking…'

'There's too much traffic,' Zoe said.

'It's rush hour. I'm sure it will clear soon. I would also like to stretch my wheels.'

29

'We've been here forever,' said Vincent.

'There has been an accident on the A47. Delays are to be expected…' cut in the GPS.

'Hm. Let me see. Not quite. It's not an accident. There has been a breakdown,' said Merida. 'I dislike GPSs. They always get it wrong.'

'I'm going to have a breakdown soon,' Lizzie muttered. She paused. 'How did you know about the Astra slide in York?'

'I searched the internet,' Merida said.

'Oh so you're not that clever, Merida,' Lizzie muttered.

'Is there internet?' Vincent called. 'Can we download apps?'

'Yes, there's internet, Vincent,' Merida replied. 'But only for me. The Electro Magnetic Field can be bad for young brains. As is too much time on the iPad. They are very addictive.'

'What's that mean?' Vincent asked.

'It means that they might create roads in your brain to bad places. Roads that are bumpy and dangerous.'

'Oh, okay. But can I download the aeroplane app? There's no roads in that. Only runways.'

'That might be useful,' Merida said. 'But, first, perhaps you'd like to see some magic?'

Chapter 4 – Magic

'Yes!' yelled Zoe and Vincent.

'That would be good,' said Lizzie. 'Particularly if it involves getting rid of the traffic.'

'I couldn't do that, Lizzie! Where would it go?'

'I don't know. I thought you said you could do magic,' Lizzie said.

'Of course, but I couldn't hurt anyone. I can only do magic to myself.' Merida paused. 'First of all, I need it not to rain again. If it rains it might not work. And, Vincent, you need to put that iPad away. It affects my concentration.'

Vincent slammed the cover shut. Zoe felt butterflies fluttering about in her tummy. Something BIG was going to happen. She felt it. This was amazing. She hadn't even thought about Lilly's shoes for ages. Even her mum was being amazing.

'It's stopped raining now,' Lizzie said.

'Yes, and it looks like it might be clear for the next half an hour,' Merida said. 'Are we ready? It can be quite noisy.'

'Can we come and sit in the front?' Zoe asked her mother. Both she and her mother looked surprised: Zoe didn't normally ask.

'Are the airbags deactivated?' Lizzie checked with Merida.

'Hm. I don't have any airbags,' Merida said. 'I only have inflatables. So that's lucky.'

Lizzie nodded. Zoe and Vincent scrambled to the front and put the seatbelt round them.

'Are you ready?' Merida asked.

'Yes!' said Zoe and Vincent.

Lizzie didn't say anything.

'Lizzie, put the gear into "A" or "ME" please,' Merida asked.

'What's the difference?'

'"A" is for Automatic, "ME" is for me, of course,' Merida said.

No one asked what that meant exactly.

Lizzie sat back down and pressed the "A". 'Like that?'

'Perfect. Now you don't have to do anything. Keep your hands off the steering wheel and your feet off the pedals. Okay?'

'Not really,' said Lizzie.

'Now can you press "I". Lizzie looked around the dashboard and found "I" and pressed it.'

Something clamped to the sides of the camper. Over the windscreen a light mesh screen dropped down.

'What is it?' Zoe asked.

'It's an invisible coat!' said Vincent.

'You are a clever boy, Vincent. And well done, Lizzie. Trust is a big thing and …'

Merida's words were lost to the sound of an enormous engine. Something clunked and clanked, stirred and whirred on top of the camper until it settled into a rhythmic wap.

WAP-WAP-WAP-WAP-WAP-WAP-WAP-WAP.

'It's like a helicopter!' Vincent shouted. 'An invisible helicopter!'

'Very clever indeed,' Merida shouted.

'Oh my goodness!' Lizzie shouted. 'What's happening?'

'It's okay, Lizzie. Please trust me.'

Cars and lorries started beeping their horns and flashing their lights at them.

'Can they see us?' Zoe asked.

'No we've disappeared. But we're still here of course. And now...'

'Oh my goodness...Oh NO!'

The campervan rose up into the air above the traffic. It hovered on the spot for a few seconds before turning and flying over the cars and lorries crouched on the road like little shiny beetles, one behind the other, waiting. Some people were getting out and gesticulating to where the campervan had been. Several heads turned upwards. More followed. Zoe's mouth fell open and her stomach rose up. She swallowed. They were flying. Invisibly. No one could see them. How amazing was that.

WAP-WAP-WAP-WAP-WAP-WAP-WAP-WAP.

Vincent waved to them. No one waved back. Confused faces searched the clouds above them.

'Wow!' said Zoe. 'We're flying!'

In a few minutes they had left the traffic jams behind them.

'Are you okay, Mummy?' Zoe asked.

'Yes, fine.' Lizzie had turned very pale.

'Look, down there! Jumping cows,' Vincent said, pointing.

'And the horses are running!' Zoe said.

'Animals sense things more than humans,' Merida explained.

'Look at the train! It's running away!' Vincent said, laughing. Zoe laughed, too. Vincent said really funny things sometimes. It was because he was only seven.

'We're going to have to land soon,' said Merida. 'We make too much noise and we could be picked up on radars. I hear Norfolk has a lot of radars. Besides, it's getting dark. It could start raining any moment.'

'What happens in the rain?' Zoe asked.

'Well, I'm afraid the invisibility shield doesn't work so well. You see, to become invisible – or, at least, one way to become invisible – is to bend light. The shield is designed to not cause shadows. But water distorts light and all sorts of strange things might happen. Also the solar panels are not as effective and, of course, we need power to make us invisible.'

'I know that,' said Vincent.

'No you don't, Vincent.' Zoe said. 'No one knows that.'

'I do know that. When you put a stick in water it bends.'

'That's right, Vincent,' Merida said.

'Goodness, Vincent, you are clever,' said Lizzie. 'I wouldn't have thought of that.'

Zoe elbowed Vincent for being so clever.

'How do you fly?' Lizzie asked. 'Really.'

'By magic of course,' Zoe said.

'Not exactly. I have tandem rotor blades. Like a mini Chinook helicopter. The one in front is smaller than the rear one. The blades fold up in the boxes on my roof.'

'What does "tandem" mean?' Zoe asked.

'It means 'together',' Merida explained. 'Maybe you've seen a tandem bike – built for two people?'

'Yes, I know,' said Vincent.

Zoe stared at him, narrowing her eyes like her mother did to her when she was cross. He ignored her.

'We'll fly over the Wash and land near Skegness,' said Merida. 'We can find a campsite to stay. According to the GPS there's plenty – and almost no people at the end of April.'

Lights in houses and village street lights started switching on across the land. The sky, stuffed with heavy clouds, hung heavily above them while the darkening land

34

gave way to a broad band of golden and then the darkening sea. Zoe watched out the window as they flew over the sea to the other side and landed on a remote country road in rural Lincolnshire.

Chapter 5 – Ely's escape from Balli

From inside the Volkswagen Polo, Ely could hear the sound of a helicopter wapping above her. She searched the sky out of the side window above her, but although she could see the clouds moving, she couldn't see anything. She waited until the driver had gone into the cottage and the door slammed shut before unfolding herself from behind the driver's seat and clicking open the car door. No one. It was clear. A street light flicked on. There was no way Balli could have followed her. She let out a sigh of relief and stepped out into the damp grass, crouching low. She guessed she must be somewhere in England. The driver had spoken English on the phone and she knew that Balli went to England often. Behind her, all she could see was a narrow lane dotted with cottages and lots of green fields. The sky was darkening and the smell of salt lingered in the air. They were not so far from the sea. The helicopter now wapped in the distance but she still couldn't see it. It was nothing.

Bali had captured her on his mountain in Iceland where she had gone in search of her best friend and her friend's mother who had disappeared. She had not expected him to be there and had not bothered to wear her cloak which was folded up and tucked in a deep inside pocket of her sky-blue jacket. He had come up behind her in the middle of the afternoon as the sun pelted the ice, turning it into puddles of water, and had thrown a stinking blanket over her head so she could neither see, nor scream. The stench of unwashed clothes and dead animals crept up her nose and down to her stomach.

'You as well!' he'd growled. 'HOW DARE YOU?'

'I...I... I...come... for Dana.' Ely felt sick.

'She did not read the signs. She was trespassing, like you! HOW DARE YOU COME ONTO MY LAND?'

He pushed her into the snow and had shouted so loudly that she heard the cracking of ice.

'NOW look what you've made me do, you interfering rotten piece of puffin. I will throw you overboard and feed you to the sharks like the others.'

He had dragged her through the snow and ice for hours until she finally found herself locked into a dark metal container. He bound her hands together and threatened to keep her imprisoned forever – or throw her overboard. He left her in the dark and cold. Before long, she had felt the movement of the sea. Up and down. Up and down.

She was lucky. The sea was too rough for him to take her on deck to throw her overboard. She curled up in a corner, closed her eyes and breathed deeply. She had no food or water, other than the melting snow that had blown into the trailer. She could hear the screech of seagulls. They were heading south-east, she thought.

After what felt like many days, the boat creaked to a halt. She felt weak and could hardly get herself up but she knew she must stay alert. Then, at the port, he had made a mistake. He was asked to show documents and sign customs papers. They told him to open up his truck. He had warned her in Icelandic to keep quiet. She knew that this was her chance. She wondered if she should reveal herself and tell her she'd been kidnapped but she knew that he would say she was a stowaway and that would be worse for her. No. Instead, she wriggled her tiny hands out of her coat and the ropes around her wrists, took out her cloak and hid behind the door, leaving her coat in the corner. As the officials entered the container and had their backs to her, she crept out, unnoticed. Darting from car to car in the terminal she found the old VW with an open back door. She slipped in it and pulled the door closed. On the floor she found a bottle of water. She opened it and drank thirstily. The driver came back, got in and drove off. She estimated he had driven for about two hours. She could be anywhere. For sure, she was a long way from home and she had no idea how she would get back. Or where her friends were. Had he really thrown them overboard?

She pushed the car door shut and crept along the side of the hedge. The helicopter had stopped wapping and yet she could feel a presence. It was a powerful presence. Ely had never felt anything quite like it. It was as if she was pushing through a magnetic field, massaged by positive and negative ions. Headlights came towards her. The rumble of a deep-throated motor. Before she knew what she was doing, she found herself taking off her cloak and stepping out into the road like a moth driven towards light.

Chapter 6 – A Child in the Road

'Look! There's a child in the road!' Zoe said, pointing to a very little person. She, if it was a she, looked like she had just crawled out of a bush. She was taking off an almost transparent mesh garment that looked like a cloak with a large hood, and was standing in the middle of the road.

'She needs our help,' Merida said.

Lizzie pulled over and opened the window. Zoe leaned over and looked out. The little girl did not even reach the window.

'Hello. Are you all right?'

The little girl looked at them and smiled. She was no bigger than Vincent, perhaps even smaller, but definitely older. She had long silky dark hair, a bit like Zoe's when she washed it, dark eyes, pale skin and wore tight blue trousers, red laced-up boots and a red, baggy, long-sleeve shirt with hundreds of red and silver sequins that twinkled in the light. She must be freezing.

'Yes, I'm alive, thank you. Just a bit lost. And hungry. Where am I?' The girl spoke softly, slowly.

'Lincolnshire. Near Skegness,' said Lizzie.

Zoe could tell the girl had never heard of Lincolnshire. Vincent got up and opened a cupboard.

'Why are you on your own?' her mother asked. 'Vincent, sit down please.'

Vincent continued to rummage about in the cupboard, taking things out.

'A long story but I've just escaped from a very nasty troll.'

'A troll?' said Lizzie. 'What do you mean? A troll? There are no such things as trolls. Only in books.'

Zoe sighed. Adults again. They didn't believe anything.

'Where I come from they're everywhere. We try to keep out of their way and normally they don't hurt us but they are angry creatures and one got cross with me, captured me, and smuggled me on a ship. I escaped at the port.'

'Goodness. Where are you from?'

'From the north. Near Tröllaskagi. Iceland.'

'Iceland?'

Her mother sounded surprised. Zoe too. Why would the little girl come from a supermarket?

'Here!' said Vincent, leaning over Lizzie to hand the girl a packet of salt and vinegar crisps, a bread roll, some ham and a yoghurt. He also took off his red and pink jumper and gave it to her. Underneath he was wearing his 'Messy Hair, Don't Care' shirt.

Zoe swallowed. She could have given the girl something.

'Thank you. Where are you going?' the little girl asked, slipping the jumper on and taking the items, one by one.

'To the fastest slide in the world!' Zoe declared. 'Here, have a bag.' She grabbed a paper bag that was on the floor.

'Oh, yes, thank you. Where's that?'

'York.'

'I've never heard of York.' She paused. 'I'm fairly sure that it isn't the fastest slide though.'

'Would you like to come with us?' Vincent asked.

Zoe looked at her mother. She wasn't going to like that. Zoe was right. Her mother was frowning.

'Well, we're not going yet,' Lizzie explained. 'We're going to a campsite to sleep. Perhaps we could…'

'Oh please don't worry about me. I have some food now. Thank you. I'll be fine. Thank you, Vincent and Zoe.'

'But…'

But the little girl opened up her cloak, stepped back towards the hedge and disappeared.

Everyone was quiet. Their eyes roamed the road and fields for her but she'd quite simply vanished.

'Where is she?' Vincent asked.

Merida didn't say anything. Lizzie started the campervan.

'I was going to say we would take her to the campsite with us.'

'She could feel your hesitation, Lizzie,' Merida said. 'Some people, especially little people, feel more than others because they haven't yet learned how not to. They haven't blocked their feelings.' Merida paused. 'Don't worry, it's not your fault.'

Vincent and Zoe were still quiet.

'Perhaps I should call the police,' Lizzie muttered to herself.

'And say what? A little girl disappeared in front of us? If she can disappear like that, she can look after herself.'

The GPS took them to a small campsite near the sea. Her mother checked them in and then parked up. Vincent helped Lizzie plug up to the mains and the inside of the campervan came alive. Lights flashed on, the fridge hummed, the kettle sang, the hot water gurgled, and hot air blasted out of vents.

'Wow, there's even central heating!' Lizzie exclaimed. She closed all the blinds and pulled down the bed from the roof. 'Now, how do I make these seats into a bed?'

'There's a button on the side of the window that says B2,' Merida explained.

'Here it is!' said Vincent, pushing it.

The table and chairs clunked into a bed.

'That is magic!' said Lizzie.

'Good. I think I will have a sleep now,' Merida said. 'I'm tired after all that flying and you're all safe on the campsite.'

Within seconds Merida started snoring.

Vincent and Zoe started laughing.

'Shall we switch her off?' Lizzie said.

But they all decided they wanted to leave her on. Just in case.

Chapter 7 – Mary Poppins and Rubbish

The next morning, Zoe woke up in an upsteps bed next to Milly Monkey, Chipeto the donkey and Vincent. She felt warm and cosy. Outside she could hear the sea crashing. A seagull called to her: O-ee, O-ee! They were in a campsite near the sea, on their way to the fastest slide in the world.

'Wake up, Zoe and Vincent,' said Merida. 'It's eight o'clock! Come on, Lizzie, you too.'

Her mother yawned somewhere down below. Zoe peered down to see her mother stretching her arms up-up-up. She was smiling.

'Goodness me! Is that the time? That was the best sleep I've had in years! Even with you snoring, Merida.'

'I don't snore.'

'Yes you do!' Zoe and her mother shouted.

'Absolutely not. Campervans don't snore. I heard nothing. Anyway, we'd better get going if we want to get to York today. I've checked the GPS and it's still going to take three hours. And the GPS is bound to be wrong.'

'Can we fly?' Zoe said.

'Oh no,' Merida said. 'Flying is only for emergencies. We use too much petrol.'

'What about the solar panels?' Lizzie asked.

'I use solar for invisibility and diesel for flying. I'm quite a weight, you know. Especially with you lot on board. Besides, I need to do more exercise.'

Zoe laughed as she imagined a fat campervan. She jumped on Vincent who was still sleeping. He screamed and buried himself in his soft blue and white flecked blanket.

Lizzie flicked up the blinds and got out pans and plates to make them all scrambled eggs and beans for breakfast. They sat around the inside table to eat. A black retriever walked by, pulling an elderly man.

'Okay, kids, we'll go and have a shower and then we'll get going.'

They grabbed towels, shampoo and clean clothes, then Vincent pressed the button to swish open the campervan door. Zoe stepped down first and stopped. All around the campervan the grass lay flat as if someone, or something, had been prowling around. Round and round. Zoe hoped it wasn't the little girl. But surely Merida would have heard? Maybe not with her snoring. Her mother and Vincent were also looking.

'I thought I heard someone huffing and puffing in the night,' said Vincent.

Zoe tried to find a footprint but there was no mud, only flattened grass. When they got back from the shower, Lizzie asked Merida if she knew anything about it, if she had heard anything? Or if she had some kind of CCTV camera onboard?

Merida said she hadn't. Her headlights had been off: how could she have seen in the dark? 'But I shouldn't worry,' she added. 'No one could ever get in.'

'Well, it's a mystery,' said Lizzie. 'Maybe it was a dog sniffing around.'

No one said anything. Zoe knew it hadn't been a dog.

'Can I go on the slide?' Vincent asked her mother.

Zoe had also spotted the campsite park. And the swimming pool.

'You have ten minutes, Vincent and Zoe. I just need to pack up. So just go to the park. And stay within view. And can you comb your hair, Vincent.'

45

'Okay,' he said, walking away while running his hands through his dark curls and messing it up even more.

Zoe walked with Vincent to the slide but it was covered in decomposed leaves from the winter. Vincent climbed on a tyre hanging on a tree.

'Push me!'

Zoe pushed him, then tried to crank up a roundabout that creaked. Before long she felt hot.

'I'm going back,' she called to Vincent, who had jumped off the tyre and was picking some cowslips.

Zoe walked back to the camper. She heard voices from inside. Merida was talking. For once, her mother was quiet. Zoe stood by the open sliding door and listened.

'When you are a child...' Merida was saying, '... you soak up everything – good and bad, like a vacuum cleaner hoovering up and, mostly, it is rubbish. Whatever it is becomes hard-wired into your brains so as an adult you find yourself repeating the same rubbish. For example, you believe that children should do as they're told without questioning or explanation. That it is okay to shout at them, or even hit them. That it is normal to humiliate them. You tell them that they shouldn't fight but then they witness someone hitting you or you hitting someone, or watch people hitting each other on television. You tell them not to lie but then you lie and tell them not to say anything. Not surprisingly, that causes conflict, chaos and confusion in young people. You are telling them one thing and doing another. They can't make sense of adult behaviour and then their behaviour goes off track and they start to do things they shouldn't...'

Zoe felt something in her stomach move. She felt funny and didn't know why.

'... I don't know what your past was like, Lizzie, and, in a way, it doesn't matter. For sure, you hoovered up some bad stuff that you are passing on to Zoe. But it is important to remember that you aren't to blame. It's what you learned from your parents. Neither were your parents to blame. They were only repeating what they had learned. And the generation before. And so on and so on and so on, back and back. Generations of rubbish passed on from adult to child. So it is not your fault. You have been handed down a suitcase full of rubbish. Let it go. It's not yours. It was given to you. The little Lizzie never asked for it. Get rid of it before you pass on any more to Zoe.'

'What rubbish?' Zoe asked, unable to keep still any longer. 'Pass on what? I don't understand.' Her mother had never kept quiet for so long.

Her mother smiled at her. Also unusual.

'Hello darling, we're just talking about how we pass on rubbish to our children.'

'Like that rubbish DVD about a woman who flies with an umbrella you gave to me?'

'Mary Poppins? Not exactly.'

'In a way, Zoe is right,' said Merida. 'That is rubbish. The mother is not really interested in looking after the children and their previous nanny blames them for their bad behaviour. What kind of example is that? It's not exactly building the children's confidence. It's rubbish.'

'It was boring,' Zoe said.

'It is dated,' Lizzie said. 'There is a new version. Anyway, I'm ready. Except for disconnecting the electricity. And taking the rubbish to the bin.' She laughed, a spring in her stride as she jumped out of the camper with the plastic bag.

47

'What were you talking about to Mummy?' Zoe asked Merida.

'I was just trying to help her understand why she sometimes gets angry with you or blames you for something. That's not right. But it's not her fault. And it is certainly not your fault. She has learned those reactions from her parents and the people around her when she was younger. If she can let go of that rubbish she has been given she can change her reactions. She needs to connect to you.' Merida paused. 'But it is not easy. Children can be very annoying.' She laughed. 'But, really, all children are good but they need and deserve the love, support and attention of a tribe.'

'What's a tribe?' Zoe asked, reddening. She wasn't good. Merida didn't know how naughty she was. She didn't know she had pinched that girl. And hidden her shoes.

'A tribe is a group of people who live together and share responsibilities and duties. For example, some people may go shopping, other people may do the cooking. Everyone looks after the children.'

'Oh,' she said. She didn't know any tribes in Norwich. And, thinking about it, she'd rather be with her mum than with a whole group of people.

'But it is my fault if I hit someone. Mummy always tells me not to hit.'

'It is wrong to hit,' Merida said. 'And you need to learn that. But forgive yourself. You are learning. It is normal for a child to play fight but if a child is very aggressive, hitting a lot, it is perhaps because he or she is, or has, experienced aggression at home. Or at school. Maybe someone is hitting her. Being bullied.'

Zoe reddened again as she thought of Sheena.

48

'It may even have been before the child remembers. No child deserves to be hit or hurt.'

Zoe was about to ask if pinching counted but her mum and Vincent came back. Vincent carried a bunch of yellow cowslips. He gave half to her and half to her mum.

'Thank you, Vincent. That's very kind. Zoe, can you get a little cup of water?'

Zoe was about to moan but, instead, she got two cups of water for the yellow flowers and put them on the table.

Everyone binged in their seatbelts.

Lizzie started the engine. 'Okay, A16, followed by A18.'

Vincent had a new app about building bridges that he started doing. Zoe thought it looked very difficult.

'Vincent's on the iPad again,' she said.

'Half an hour is okay,' her mother said. Merida didn't say anything.

Zoe looked out of the window. Her mum did shout. And she had smacked her. But only when she was very very naughty. But Merida had said that her mother's behaviour was not always good. Zoe knew that. She blamed Zoe for everything – even when they were late for school and Zoe had been waiting by the door for half an hour. But Merida had also said that it wasn't her mother's fault either. It was her grandparents. And it wasn't their fault either. Hm. Zoe wasn't sure about that. And what about burying that girl's shoes? Whose fault was that? And, if pinching counted, what about pinching that girl? She couldn't really blame her nana for that. Or Sheena. Could she? Maybe she could. She wasn't sure but she was starting to feel better. She read a sign, 'S-c-u-n-th-or-pe'.

'Scunthorpe,' her mother said. 'Well done.'

Zoe felt good. She read the next one: GRIM-S-BYE!' She laughed.

49

'Grimsby.'

'Bee?' Zoe sighed. Silly spelling again.

'It's old English,' her mother said.

'When will it be new English?' Zoe asked.

'It could do with updating.'

They drove along in silence for a while – except for the sound of Vincent's bridges crashing. Zoe stared at the large stretch of white dough pulled across the sky. Just occasionally she could see blue. Merida was very quiet. Zoe checked the green light was on.

'Are you there, Merida?' she asked.

'Yes, Zoe. I'm feeling a little tired though.'

Zoe thought that odd but no one said anything. Fortunately, there was little traffic and the GPS told her mum where to go: 'At the next roundabout take the second exit.'

'Lizzie, would you mind stopping?' Merida asked.

'Of course not. I'll pull in at the next service station or garage. We need some diesel anyway.'

'What's the matter?' Zoe asked.

Even Vincent looked up from his iPad.

'I'm not sure. I'm feeling heavier than usual,' Merida said.

Chapter 8 – The Rock

They crawled around an enormous roundabout and over a motorway. Lizzie pulled into a petrol station where two lorries were filling up.

'Can you just check on top of my roof, Lizzie, please,' asked Merida. If you press the button with the step on it a ladder will open up at the back.'

'I'll go!' said Vincent.

'Me too,' said Zoe.

'Okay, but first diesel.'

Zoe waited for her mum to fill up Merida and then, after they'd parked, she and Vincent jumped out of the side door and ran to the rear of the great grey shiny body.

'It's high,' Zoe said.

Vincent tried to reach the first rung but his legs were too little.

'I can do it,' said Zoe, pushing Vincent out of the way.

'No, neither of you can, it's too dangerous,' Lizzie said.

Zoe and Vincent both started to protest.

'That's a nice van you got there,' a lorry driver with orange spiky hair said, coming over to them.

'Yes, she's magic,' Vincent said. Zoe nudged him.

'She looks it. What's the problem?'

'We just wanted to check that everything's okay on the top,' Lizzie said. 'Meri… The van was feeling a bit heavy.'

'Well, I would have thought it was the motor that's the problem, not the roof! Want me to have a look?'

'No it's okay, the motor's running perfectly. I'll just have a quick look up here. See if anything's come loose.' Lizzie slowly climbed up the perpendicular ladder.

The man crouched on the floor and looked underneath the camper. Zoe flicked her eyes up and down.

'Blow me!' said the man.

'What?' said Zoe and Vincent. 'What is it?'

'It's all sealed. It looks impossible to open. There's not even any screws that I can see. It's four-wheel drive and it's got a protective shield underneath for rocks. You could drive this thing on the moon! Hold on a minute, what's this? That shouldn't be there, surely. It's not a spare wheel, I don't think, no.'

'What?' asked Lizzie, coming down the ladder.

'It looks like a very big stone has got lodged in the chassis.' The man grunted several times as he wriggled further underneath Merida. 'Ahhh. Come on, shift. No, it's stuck solid.'

The man's boots reappeared from underneath the van. Followed by his now dirt-streaked jeans, and blue denim jacket and, finally, his red face. A leaf stuck in his red hair. He got up. 'I'll go and get a crowbar from my lorry,' he said.

'What's a crowbar?' Vincent asked, when the man had gone.

'It's for crows to sit on, silly,' said Zoe.

'Not quite. It's a kind of metal stick with a thinner rounded end to pry things apart,' Lizzie explained. 'I don't know where the word comes from.'

'Maybe they look like crows,' said Zoe.

Her mum smiled at her. 'Maybe.'

Vincent looked underneath. Zoe heard something scrabbling around.

Vincent screamed. 'Something just ran off!' he said, pointing to the right side of the camper.

'Don't be silly,' said Lizzie.

'Yes, it did! Over there!'

Zoe thought she saw a dark shadow darting between the lorries. Vincent ran after it.

'Vincent! Come back!' Lizzie ran after him and grabbed his hand.

'But it went over there!' Vincent protested.

The man came back with a crowbar and shuffled under the van again.

'Well, blow me,' he said. 'It's gone!'

Vincent started crying. 'I told you, I saw it!'

'How could a rock run?' Lizzie said. She turned to the man. 'Are you sure it was a rock? Could it have been a stowaway?'

'No way! It was solid. As a rock! It was lumpy. It had no legs!'

'Well, there's a mystery. But it's gone now.'

The man paused. 'Where are you people from?' Suspicion narrowed his eyes.

'Norwich,' Lizzie replied.

'And where are you going?'

'York.'

'We're going to the fastest slide in the world,' Zoe added.

'The biggest indoor slide in the UK,' her mother corrected. 'It's an adventure play area.'

'Oh, well, have a good time,' the man said.

'Thank you for your help,' said Lizzie.

'Where are you going?' asked Vincent.

'Oh, I'm catching a cargo boat from Immingham to Esbjerg. Denmark, that is.'

He shook his head and the leaf fell out, then he went off to his lorry.

Zoe and Vincent got back into the camper. Lizzie swished the door closed and sat down at the driver seat and pressed 'M'.

'That's better,' Merida said. 'What was it?'

'A little round man. He was underneath you,' Vincent said.

'Vincent, we're not sure,' Lizzie said. 'A lorry driver said that it was a large stone.'

'But then it ran away. I saw it!'

'Hm. But at least it's gone. I feel much better already. Let's go.'

Lizzie started the engine and Merida raced forward.

'Hey, steady on.'

'Oh, much better,' Merida tooted as she slalomed a roundabout.

'I wonder who it was,' Zoe said.

'I don't know,' Lizzie said.

'I think it was the troll,' Vincent said quietly.

'I'm afraid I think you're right, Vincent,' said Merida.

Silence.

'There's no such thing as trolls,' Lizzie said.

'Perhaps it depends on your definition of "troll",' said Merida. 'Whoever it was he was as heavy as rock.' She chuckled and refused to say any more on the subject.

Chapter 9 – The Campsite

It was lunchtime by the time they reached the outskirts of York. Church spires poked the greying clouds.

'I think we're going to pass the campsite soon.' Lizzie turned into the campsite and parked near the reception. Several campers walked by, one was carrying a bucket, another a Jack Russell dog. They didn't look very happy. The one with the dog scowled at Zoe.

'What about Merida?' Vincent said. 'Can she come with us to the slide?'

'Don't be silly, Vincent. She's a campervan!'

'Oo-oh,' Vincent and Zoe chimed.

'Merrida chuckled. 'Have you ever seen a campervan on a slide?'

'But you could take us,' Vincent insisted.

'Well, I could but…'

'We can get the bus. It's only down the road. Once we're hooked up at a campsite we can't really drive. Now wait here a minute. I will go and check in.' Lizzie opened the driver's door and jumped down.

'Can't you fly in, Merida?' Vincent whispered.

'Yes, go on, Merida!' Zoe said. Merida made her feel safe, protected. Zoe reckoned, if she did have another parent, she would like one like Merida. One that flew. And one that could be invisible. That would be so cool.

'Remember,' Merida said, 'I only ever fly when there is no reasonable alternative. And I only float when I have absolutely no other alternative. I dislike water, particularly cold water, very much.'

'But water slides are the best!' said Vincent. 'I like them so much.'

'That's because you're a little boy, Vincent. I'm a van. There's a difference.'

Vincent paused.

'Which is fastest: wind or a cheetah?'

'It depends how fast the wind is blowing. The maximum wind gust that has been recorded is 253 mph. But that was a gust. Cheetahs can reach about 75mph.'

'How fast can you go?'

'About 100 mph.'

'Wow. How about when you fly?' Vincent asked.

'About the same.'

'Vincent?' Zoe asked. 'Do you think Merida is like a mum?' she asked. 'Or a dad?'

Vincent laughed. 'That's silly! Daddies are men.'

Merida chuckled. Zoe thought the van moved a little but maybe that was her imagination.

'Vincent is right. I'm a van not a man. But I was made by a very wise man so maybe you're a little bit right, Zoe.'

'You're not like my daddy,' Vincent whispered.

'No, Vincent, probably not. Most fathers don't know how to be fathers because they didn't have good fathers. It's not their fault. But I think your mum is a good mum. One good parent is better than two rubbish ones.'

'But not as good as two or three good ones,' Vincent said.

'True.'

'Three!' Zoe said. Three parents? Silly Vincent.'

Just then Lizzie's angry shouts could be heard from the reception. She shot out of the door with a red face. She climbed into the driver's seat and started Merida.

'Mummy!' Zoe stared as her mother pressed the 'I' button.

'Sorry, Merida, we have to disappear. It's an emergency.'

'Very well, Lizzie.'

The shield clamped around the van and the mesh screen zipped down the window and in less than five seconds they were invisible. The man dropped his dog and stood, opened-mouthed, at the space where the campervan had been. The dog yapped.

'Do you want to fly?' Merida asked calmly.

'No, that's not necessary,' said Lizzie, rounding her arms on the steering wheel.

'I think it is,' said Merida.

A Hymer mobile home driven by a round bald man trundled towards them. A group of campers gathered around. Some were pointing to where they had been. Zoe wondered what had got into her mother.

'Oh plonkers.'

The boxes clunked open on the roof and, presumably, the blades unfolded. The motors growled like a hundred tigers. A woman screamed and pointed to where the noise was coming from.

WAP-WAP-WAP-WAP-WAP-WAP-WAP-WAP.

'Mummy!' Zoe yelled.

They lifted up just as the Hymer passed beneath them.

'Sorry, everyone,' her mother said. 'Thank you, Merida.'

'What happened?' Merida asked.

'Oh nothing much,' Lizzie said.

'Nothing much! You nearly killed us for nothing much!' Zoe couldn't believe her mother. She was acting differently. More in charge. But completely bonkers. Zoe didn't know whether she should gain stars – or lose them.

'What happened?' Merida asked again.

'Oh they just said that children and magic campervans weren't allowed in. I mean it's a campsite, for goodness sake! How can you forbid children from a campsite? Sorry, it made me cross.'

'Oh never mind,' said Merida, curving round to the right. 'There are lots of silly people and silly rules in the world. Don't get cross. It's not worth it. You only hurt yourself. And might kill us.'

'Hm. Yes, you're right. Sorry, everyone.'

Zoe felt herself tipping as if they were on a fairground ride on one of those chairs that fly out. She had to hold on.

'What are you doing, Merida?' Lizzie asked.

They were hovering above the campsite. The campers were coming out of their mobile homes looking up, petrified. Some covered their ears. The dog had disappeared.

'Oh, I just thought we should go and say sorry to them. I mean they have to live with themselves.'

59

Merida went even closer so that hats blew off and shirts blew up. Blades of grass shivered. One held up a camera or a mobile phone.

'Can they see us?'

'No. But they can hear us, of course.'

'Sorry!' called Lizzie.

'Bye-bye,' Zoe shouted, waving.

'Bye!' screamed Vincent.

Merida swung round and up and they all fell back into their chairs, laughing.

'Mummy!' Zoe said, smiling.

'Where to now?' Merida asked.

'The slide!' cried Zoe and Vincent.

Chapter 10 – The Enormous Slide

'It's going to be difficult to land,' said Merida. 'It's Saturday and we're in a city. Everyone can hear us, remember. But I'll try.'

Zoe could see everyone craning their necks to look for them in the sky and then frowning when they couldn't. Some were pointing. Cars pulled over to the side of the road.

'We're causing too much attention. We can't land here.'

Merida flew higher and higher. The church spires became needles, the houses became matchstick boxes, lakes became puddles, trees became blades of grass and fields became a patchwork quilt of greens, browns and purples.

'Okay, now we can land,' Merida said finally.

'It looks beautiful,' said Lizzie.

Merida headed down and landed on a road that cut through an enormous swathe of purple. The engines roared and then went quiet. The blades clunked back into their box on the roof. Lizzie switched off the 'I' button and the shields slid up.

'Where are we?' Zoe asked. The purple carpet rolled into the grey sky.

'Yorkshire Moors,' said Lizzie. 'The purple flowers are heather.'

'But where's the slide?' Vincent asked.

'We have to drive back,' Merida said.

They drove back into York. Several police cars passed them. Rain started spitting on the camper.

'I'm not sure it's a good idea to stay here,' Merida said. 'They may have our registration plate number. And, in the rain, we cannot disappear so easily.'

Zoe thought that Merida sounded worried.

'But I've promised the kids. I don't want to let them down.'

'Well, you've promised to take them to the fastest slide…' Merida said.

'There it is!' said Vincent, pointing.

Zoe's heart thumped at the sight of the huge posters of the indoor slide and the outside adventure park. There were even little cars to ride on.

'I want the red one!' she said.

'No, I want the red one!'

Lizzie turned into the car park and found a parking space.

'Okay, here we are,' Merida said. 'Have a good time and don't be too long.'

Zoe was not listening. She couldn't wait to go in. She crouched under an umbrella with her mum and Vincent and they all ran to the entrance. The outside park was closed because of the rain but it didn't matter as the inside soft play was open and there was The Enormous Slide. Zoe hardly heard her mother say that she would be waiting here at this table and that they should come back for a drink… as she kicked off her shoes and clambered up the red and blue steps that led up the yellow tunnel. Vincent snapped at her heels as they climbed through some red hoops, bounced through blue barricades, over a net bridge, up more platforms in a tower until they reached the top of the pink and purple slide. Then there they were. Finally. At the top of the fastest slide in England.

'Vincent. You go there!' Zoe pointed to one of the four lanes that waved down and down and down and down.

Zoe plonked herself down at the top, pushed herself off and gently sailed all the way down, up and over the purple waves.

'It's rubbish,' said Vincent, ramming her, head first.

'Ouch. Vincent! It's better than the one in Norwich. Let's go again.'

They clambered, bounced and crawled their way back up to the top.

'Hey look! There's that girl again!' Vincent cried, pointing to the bottom.

Chapter 11 – The Girl Again

Zoe turned to where Vincent was looking. He was right. The little girl in blue trousers, red boots and Vincent's red and pink jumper waved to them from the bottom. Three large plastic boards, one red, one green and one purple, rested against her legs.

Zoe and Vincent pushed themselves down the slide.

'There you are,' she said. 'I've been waiting for you.'

'Oh,' said Zoe.

'Zoe!' her mother called. 'Come and have some water please.'

Zoe and Vincent went over to where her mother was sitting. The girl went with them. She was no taller than Vincent. In other words, tiny. But she, somehow, looked old.

'Hello again,' said her mother, smiling. 'How did you get here?'

The little girl shrugged.

'What's your name?' her mother tried again.

'Ely.'

Lizzie introduced them. Ely nodded. She turned to Zoe and Vincent. 'You said you wanted to go to the fastest slide in the world, didn't you? Well, this isn't it. Would you like to go to a faster one? I've bought these.' She indicated the boards.

'Yes!' said Vincent and Zoe.

'Where to?' asked Lizzie. 'Would you like help?' She took two of the boards from Ely, which were almost as big as her. 'These look more like sledges!'

'Thank you, Lizzie. They are. I'll explain on the way. But we need your camper to get there.'

64

'I can't imagine where you plan to go,' Lizzie said. 'Mind you, it's cold enough to snow.'

They left the adventure park together and went back to Merida.

'I'm pleased you're back,' said Merida. 'A police officer has been nosing around.'

'Oh you talk as well as fly and hide,' Ely said. 'No wonder you have such a powerful energy field around you.'

Merida chuckled.

'That's Merida,' said Vincent, kneeling down in his chair. Ely nodded and said something but Zoe didn't understand what she said. She thought it was another language. Maybe Portuguese or Spanish. Zoe sat down next to Vincent. She could hardly wait to see where they were going to. Where could the biggest slide in the world be? She did her seatbelt up without being asked. Ely sat at the front.

Lizzie started the engine.

'So, where to?'

'Tröllaskagi.'

'Sorry?' Lizzie said.

'Tröllaskagi. In Iceland. It's where the biggest slide is.'

'Sorry?' said Lizzie again.

'No Iceland no!' Zoe said. No shopping.

'No no,' echoed Vincent.

Ely looked at them surprised. 'You don't want to go to a snow slide.'

'Yes!' chorused Zoe and Vincent.

'No no!' Lizzie said. 'How would we get there?'

'Merida? Will you take us?'

'No no. We can go to Edinburgh and you can catch a proper aeroplane. I'll wait for you there.'

'But we want to go to the fastest slide right?' Ely said.

'Yes!' cried Zoe and Vincent again. Zoe felt her eyes stretch open and her lips formed a big smile. A snow slide on a mountain. Wow! She loved snow more than anything.

'Well, we need Merida to take us there. It's up an ice mountain.'

An ice mountain! Zoe's heart skied up to her head.

'It's too far for me,' said Merida. 'I wouldn't have enough fuel. And way too cold.'

'If we fill up in the Faroe Islands I think you will have. Check the internet and see.'

Everyone waited for Merida's answer. Zoe held her breath and counted: one, two, three, four, five...

'We saw the troll,' Vincent said.

Ely whipped her head round to Vincent.

... seven, eight... Zoe stopped counting.

'Well, we don't know that, Vincent,' Lizzie said. She explained how Merida had felt heavy so they had stopped at a service station and how a lorry driver had found a hard rock lodged in the chassis under the van. A rock that had suddenly disappeared.

'It was a troll,' said Vincent. 'I saw it! It ran off.'

'It was a troll all right,' Ely said. 'Where did he go? Did you see?'

'Towards a big bridge,' said Vincent.

Zoe didn't know what he was talking about. She hadn't seen a bridge but Ely nodded. She looked worried.

'He must have followed me,' she said. 'Well, hopefully, we'll get there before he does. You see, the fastest slide is on his mountain. Merida? Can you do it?'

'I'm still calculating,' Merida replied.

'I... also need to get back home. I could try to get on a ship but it wouldn't be easy and I'm afraid he will follow me and lock me up again. And I cannot take a normal aeroplane. I don't have a passport. Or money. Will you do it?'

Merida was silent again.

This time everyone held their breath.

… nine, ten… Zoe finished counting.

'Okay,' said Merida. 'But it's going to be close.'

Lizzie sighed and got back into the driver's seat. She looked at the GPS. 'I'm not sure about this. Where do we need to go to?'

'North,' said Merida. 'We just drive north. We will get to the nearest point and then we will fly.'

Lizzie hummed and hawed and spelt E-D-I-N-B-U-R-G-H. That was worse than 'Norwich'. Zoe wondered why it wasn't spelled 'Edinburra'. Or maybe Edinburrah if they wanted to make it complicated. But 'burgh'? Spelling in English – even if it was old – was the silliest thing in the world.

Lizzie turned out of the adventure park just as a police car turned in.

'Oh dear…' said Lizzie. 'I think they might be onto us.'

'Keep going,' said Merida. 'Whatever you do, don't go invisible.'

'It's turned round and is following us.'

Police sirens shrieked behind them and blue flashing lights crept past and pulled them in. Her mother's finger hesitated on the 'I' button.

'No, Mummy.'

Lizzie pulled in behind the police car and wound down the window. Two police officers came towards them. One of them disappeared around the side of the van. The other one came to the window. His moustache reminded Zoe of Barnacles from Octonauts. Zoe had liked him when she was younger. Barnacles glanced inside the camper. Zoe smiled sweetly and held onto Vincent's hand. She couldn't see Ely.

'Good afternoon,' he said brightly. 'How are we doing? How many have we got in here?'

'Afternoon officer,' Lizzie chirped. 'There's just me and the kids.' She glanced round and frowned. 'That's Zoe and Vincent.'

Zoe also glanced around. Ely had disappeared. She must be hiding in the toilet.

'Are they your children?'

'Zoe is, yes. Vincent is our neighbour's child. We've just come to York for the day. Have I done anything wrong, Constable erm...?'

The officer cleared his throat. 'Barney. Constable Barney. We've reports that this vehicle has been acting strangely.' He laughed. 'Witnesses said that you ... erm... disappeared!'

Lizzie laughed. 'But that's ridiculous.'

'I know but we have to check these things out. Can I see your driving licence and documents please?'

Lizzie rummaged around the glove compartment and found a green plastic file and handed the contents to the officer.

'Well, everything seems to be in order. Nice campervan you've got. Never heard of the make. Where did you get it from?'

'Er, we got it in Norwich.'

The other officer came to the window. She had round glasses and a stern gaze.

'Must have cost a lot of money...' the other officer said. 'It's almost new.'

'Yes,' said Lizzie.

'It was free!' shouted Vincent. Zoe elbowed him. She knew there were times when it wasn't quite right to tell the truth.

The police officers swivelled their heads to look at him.

'It was free, was it? Well I hope you didn't steal it,' the moustache said.

'No, someone gave it to us,' Vincent explained. 'And then we… we… give it to someone else.'

'Well, can I have it next?' The police officer's eyes moustache twitched. 'My kids'd love it.'

'Yes!' shouted Vincent.

Lizzie said nothing but smiled.

'Can we just have a look inside?' the woman asked.

'Yes, of course,' Lizzie said.

Zoe could hear the hesitation. What if they looked in the toilet? Ely must be hiding in there.

The woman opened a couple of cupboards: one with pots and pans, the other with food. Then she headed towards the toilet. Zoe felt her heart slam into her chest like thunder. BA-BANG! She didn't dare turn around. Vincent tried to look around but he still had his seat belt on.

She opened the door.

Then closed it.

And stepped out.

No one said anything.

Where had Ely gone?

'Well, all seems to be in order. Have a nice trip, kids,' said Barney, his moustache twitching.

Lizzie pressed a button and the door closed.

The other police officer said something in a hushed voice to her mother. Zoe couldn't hear what she said. Then they walked away.

Chapter 13 – Ely's Magic Cloak

Lizzie pulled out and back onto the ring road. Zoe looked behind. The officers had got back into their car and were watching them. Everyone started talking at once.

'What did she say, Mummy?'

'Where's Ely?' Vincent asked.

'I don't know. I thought she went to the toilet.' Lizzie breathed out. 'They said they would be watching us.'

'You did well, Lizzie,' said Merida.

'But Vincent was silly,' Zoe called out. 'He told the truth!'

'No, Vincent was right, Zoe,' Merida said. 'It's right to tell the truth.'

'But Mummy says sometimes it's better to keep quiet.'

'Sometimes it's easier to keep quiet. But it is important to tell the truth. The wonderful thing about the truth is that they wouldn't have believed it anyway.' Merida laughed.

'Where's Ely?' Vincent said again.

'I'm here,' Ely said, appearing from the back of the camper.

'Where were you?' Lizzie asked.

'I was in the toilet. You know I don't have a passport or anything.'

'But they opened the door!' Zoe said.

Ely sat down in the front passenger seat and deftly clicked in her seatbelt. Zoe wondered at how she could do things so quickly. Her long fingers seemed to have lives of their own. Everything about her was quick. And she seemed to be able to disappear quicker than Merida.

'I have this,' Ely wrapped a greeney-bluey-purplely cloak around her and vanished.

'Wow!' Zoe said.

'Wow!' said Vincent.

'What!' Lizzie said.

'It's an invisibility cloak,' Ely's voice came from the front of the van.

Lizzie's eyes searched the passenger seat for her. Zoe saw and heard the seat belt clunk in around her. It looked like it was wrapped around a ghost.

'They are becoming very popular in Iceland. I'm sure they'll catch on in England soon one day,' said Ely's voice from the front.

'That's not possible!' Lizzie exclaimed.

Zoe sighed. Adults didn't even believe what was in front of their eyes.

'You mean those things are for sale? Can you please come back, Ely. You are making me nervous.'

Ely's head reappeared floating in the front seat as she patted the hood down.

'No, all of you please.'

Ely took it off. 'The elves make them, of course. They are very expensive. And you're not allowed to wear them at school. There are serious consequences.'

'Elves?' said Zoe and her mum together.

Ely nodded.

'How does it work,' Vincent asked. 'Is it the same as Merida?'

Ely said something again in a language Zoe did not understand. Like Ely herself, it was soft, nimble and melodic. Merida responded in the same sing-song language.

'Ah yes,' Ely concluded, 'So, it is different. This cloak measures space as pixels and collects and emits light in a way so that whoever is wearing it can become invisible to the human eye.'

'Like a computer screen?'

'Yes.'

'Vincent! You are so clever.' Lizzie said, without taking her eyes off the road.

'So you have to be careful. Any part that it is not covering will be seen. So you have to cover your face. And your feet. And hands. You see this button?' Ely pointed to the top button. 'This is the one you press. On the shoulders and head are fine solar panels that power the cloak....'

'I want a go!' Vincent cried.

Ely took it off and covered Vincent in the seat. She tucked in the cloak around his head, over his black curls and around his arms and legs. Then Ely told Vincent not to move, pressed the button and Vincent disappeared.

'Goodness me!' Lizzie said, turning round.

Zoe could hardly believe it – and she was a child. She touched him. He was still there.

'I'm still here,' Vincent said. 'I can see you.'

'Of course, you're still there but you are invisible.'

'Are you sure?' Vincent asked.

'Yes,' said Ely. 'You can see but no one can see you. But if just a little piece is not covering...' She lifted up the cloak from his leg and revealed his black brushed cotton trousers and stripy red socks.

'Wow! It's my turn,' said Zoe, trying to yank it off Vincent.

'Be careful, Zoe, this is a very precious item. If you sit still I will cover you.'

Zoe frowned but sat still while Ely took it off Vincent and covered her.

'Can I press the button?' Vincent asked.

Ely let him press the button and Zoe guessed by the gasps from Vincent and her mother that she had disappeared. She could still see herself. She felt exactly the same. The material around her was like a fine mesh and there was a very slight blue-green-purple hue but, other than that, it was almost completely transparent, as if it wasn't there.

'It's strange,' she said.

'Yes,' said Ely. 'You have to remember that you are invisible. There is some discussion in Iceland about the dangers of these cloaks because no one can see you and if you forget someone could knock into you. There is also a new all-in-one suit that covers every part of your body and some boots. They sound much better as you wouldn't have to worry about your toes appearing when you walk. But I haven't tried one yet. I've only heard about them. And I imagine they are very expensive. Sometimes elves give them away – but not often.'

'Why would you want to be invisible though?' Lizzie asked. 'Surely we want to be visible? We want people to notice us!'

'Yes, you're right. It's more for dangerous situations. Walking through a park at night where there are wolves or bears, for example. Or trolls.'

'It is amazing,' said Zoe. 'I want one.' She'd be able to eat chocolate from the fridge at night without anyone seeing her.'

'I want one!' said Vincent.

'Yes, they are special, aren't they?'

'Forget it, Zoe and Vincent,' Lizzie said. 'There's no way we could buy one. And I couldn't cope with fridge doors opening by themselves.'

Zoe pouted.

Ely switched it off and took it away from Zoe. She folded it up carefully next to her.

'But, Ely, why couldn't you have got on the plane if you can be invisible?' Lizzie asked.

'Security.' Ely said. 'I would never get through.'

Zoe remembered the time they had flown to Alicante in Spain. She had had to take off her beautiful purple shoes and put them on a conveyor belt and step through a doorway that beeped as she walked out. Then someone wearing gloves had taken her to one side and wafted a long black beeping stick in front of her.

'Of course,' her mother said. 'Silly me.'

'I might have been able to get through security on a boat but it would have been risky.'

Lizzie kept driving. Vincent began playing on his iPad again. A silly game of strange structures and strange landscapes through which he had to guide a character. Zoe watched out of the window. The traffic grew sparser as they headed away from York and Merida kept on all four wheels. They passed through the purple hills. Her mother and Merida began to discuss whether they should go to Aberdeen or further. Merida preferred Peterhead which was about the furthest point they could get to on land.

Lizzie pulled over onto a hard shoulder so she could look at the map on her phone. The sky was darkening.

'Glasgow,' said Ely. 'If we take off from just outside Glasgow it will be quicker and, according to my calculations, if we fill up with fuel we will have enough to get us to the Faroe Islands.'

'It's a lot of flying,' said Merida. 'I am a campervan that flies, not an aeroplane with wheels. If we don't make it, I will have to land in the sea. And I'm definitely not a boat.'

'But you said you could go in water,' said Zoe.

75

'I wouldn't sink immediately but it wouldn't take long.'

'We will be okay,' said Ely. 'It is 435 miles or 700km. We can cover 100 miles per hour in flight mode.'

Merida was silent for a moment. She shook as a white lorry passed by. On the side was the red and orange rectangle bearing the white letters, 'Iceland'. That was an easy one. She knew 'ice' was 'ice'. Like nice. Rice. Lice. Mice. Dice. Slice. Price. Paradice. No, that last one wasn't right. Paradise was with an 's'. Zoe shook her head.

'Look! We could follow that truck!' she said. But no one was listening and Vincent was rubbish at reading. He was tapping his iPad again.

'You are right, Ely, it is possible,' said Merida.

'I'm not sure. If anything happens....' said Lizzie. 'I'm responsible for Vincent.'

Vincent looked up.

'I understand,' said Ely.

'Maybe Merida could take you,' continued Lizzie. 'We could get the train back to Norwich. After all, we've been on a very long slide in York.'

'No!' chorused Zoe and Vincent. 'We want to go too.'

Her mother tapped the steering wheel.

'If nothing goes wrong, then we should make it,' Merida said. 'Lizzie, can you stop doing that, it's giving me a headache.'

'You don't have headaches! You're a campervan. And what do you mean "if nothing goes wrong"?'

'No storms or strong winds,' Vincent said.

'No storms or strong winds,' Merida echoed. 'Thank you, Vincent.'

'I've checked the weather,' Ely said. 'It's always a little unpredictable around the Faroe Islands but it's looking good.'

Lizzie sighed. Zoe nodded at her.

'Okay, then we need the M74,' said Lizzie.

'Hooray!'

Chapter 14 – The Night Flight to the Faroe Islands

'So who is this troll?' Zoe asked, once they were smoothly humming along the roads again in the fast lane. They zipped past cars and lorries.

'His name is Balli,' Ely said, a slight tremor in her voice. 'He lives just outside the village but he controls one side of the mountains and won't let anyone on it. He puts up signs saying 'No Entry', 'Anyone daring to enter risks their life', 'Entering here will risk imprisonment' and 'No Dogs, Elves or People'.'

'Why?' said Vincent, looking up from his iPad.

'Because Balli is mean,' said Ely. 'My best friend and her mother went missing last year. Her mother works for the council and she'd been trying to persuade him that it would be good to put a gondola on the mountain so people could ski or go on the snow slide. The town needs money and a ski slope there would bring people into the valley. It's one of the few valleys with snow all year round. As you know, the glaciers are melting. It could be the longest run in Iceland – and in the world. But he got angry. Then my friend and her mother disappeared. One day when it was snowing I went onto his mountain to try to find them. I thought he wouldn't find me in the snow and, besides, I had my invisibility cloak. But the snow stopped and the sun came out and I forgot to use my cloak. He caught me and shouted at me so much that he caused an avalanche in the valley. Then, as you know, he locked me in his truck and put me on the boat to England. He had to open the container at customs and I crept out using my cloak and found an open car door. I hid there until the driver stopped – near where I met you.'

'He must have lost a star for that!' said Zoe. Balli did not sound like a nice creature. She was glad they weren't going to meet him.

'A skyful,' said Ely. She smiled at Zoe.

'And we are going to his mountain?' Lizzie asked doubtfully.

'Yes, but, don't worry, he's not there. He's here. Somewhere. I half hoped I would find my friend and her mother but I don't know where to begin to look. Or if they're alive. He said he threw them to the sharks.'

'Okay. What a charming man. What if he arrives when we are there?'

'He can't,' said Ely. 'The boat takes a long time. He will have to change at Ebsjerg or Rotterdam and wait. It could take a week or more. Some ships call in at the Faroe Islands to Akureyri. I don't know which way he will go but it will take a long time. You will be gone by then.'

'What if he flies?'

'He won't. He can't leave his truck. He brings back English black pudding amongst other things. The trolls love it.'

'Black pudding?' Lizzie sounded surprised.

Yuck. Zoe hated it. Trust a troll to like black pudding.

'And he won't know I've gone so there will be no reason to hurry back home.'

'But what will happen when he comes back?' Lizzie asked.

'Who knows?' said Ely. 'Probably more of the same.'

'Poor creature,' said Merida.

'Poor!' exclaimed Lizzie. 'He sounds horrible!'

'Indeed,' said Merida. 'Can you imagine what a horrible childhood he must have had? To want to hurt others he must have been so badly hurt. I hope I get to see him.'

79

'I don't,' said Zoe. 'He sounds scary.'

'He is. What would you do then, Merida?' Ely asked, curiously. 'What would you say to him?'

'I would say sorry; sorry that he's had such a rubbish family.'

'He's a troll! All trolls have rubbish childhoods!' Ely exclaimed.

'Exactly. I would talk to him about recycling.'

'Recycling?!' They all exclaimed.

'Yes. Each generation is recycling the same rubbish childhoods. Time to stop it. They are just passing the rubbish on, as I explained to Lizzie. Each generation of trolls is learning anger, and how to hate and hurt. It's a shame. It's just not necessary.'

Ely fell silent. Vincent was back playing on his iPad, apparently oblivious. Zoe could feel the hairs on her arms rising but she wasn't sure why. Her mother continued driving. Darkness enveloped the campervan as they continued to roll north.

'I think I should put the children to bed,' Zoe heard her mother say.

'We'll be taking off soon,' Ely replied.

'Don't you think we should wait until daytime?'

'We lose time like that,' Ely said. 'And darkness is our friend.'

Zoe wanted to say something but she felt her eyes closing.

'We need diesel before we go anywhere,' Merida said.

'Maybe we fill up now, park somewhere to rest,' Lizzie reasoned. 'Then take off at first light?'

Zoe didn't hear her mother's response but she felt Merida slow down, stopping, her mother pulling down the bed and lifting her up. She felt Vincent's soft purr next to her and she pulled her red blanket over her head and rolled to sleep as Merida soared up into the night sky and flew towards the stars.

But soon she awoke to the sound of the helicopter wap-wap-wapping against an angry wind. Rain slashed the sides and the roof. Thunder slammed down into them. She could feel them falling, buffeted by the wind. 'Higher!' someone was shouting. She felt the campervan lifting. 'We're not going to make it!' her mother cried. 'We're on red!'

'We're nearly there,' Ely said. 'I can see lights.'

Zoe sat up. 'Mummy?' she called out.

'Shush! It's all right, Zoe. We're nearly there.'

Vincent purred on, undisturbed.

'There's the petrol station,' Ely said pointing, her excitement speeding up the words. 'We need to land over there somewhere.'

As they came into land, Zoe felt the wind switch itself off. The wheels touched down onto the road and the blades clunked back into the box above her head.

'We're here,' Merida said. 'I think. It's hard to see. And just in time. I don't think we could have gone much further. I can hardly turn my wheels.'

'No, the red petrol light is flashing now,' Lizzie whispered.

Zoe crept out of bed and joined her mother and Ely at the front. The night was pitch black and blurry. Lizzie switched the engines off.

'Where are we?' Zoe asked.

'We're in the Faroe Islands,' Ely explained. 'A group of islands between Scotland and Iceland. We're just outside of Tórshavn, the main town.'

'There's nobody here,' Zoe whispered looking out into the murky night.

81

Something baaed.

'Look!'

Lizzie laughed. A flock of sheep crossed the road in front of them. One of them stopped in the middle of the road and looked at them, before hurrying across to the other side.

'Let's get petrol now,' said Ely. 'I imagine the petrol stations close before midnight.'

Lizzie started the engine again and they drove towards a small village.

'Effo,' Zoe read, and no one corrected her. A phonetic country. That was exciting.

A brightly lit petrol station came into view.

'It might be an idea if you go back into bed, Zoe. We don't want to draw attention to ourselves and it is late for a child to be up.'

Zoe found herself doing as she was told again. Strange, she thought.

Her mother pulled into the petrol station and opened the door. Ely and her mother went out.

Zoe listened to the glug-glug-glug of the petrol being pumped into Merida.

'Merida?' she whispered.

'Yes, Zoe?' Merida replied.

'I feel...' Zoe paused. 'Happy,' she said.

'Good, Zoe. There's no other way to be,' Merida said. 'When we like ourselves, we are happy. It's simple. And there's no reason not to like ourselves.'

Zoe frowned in the dark remembering the shoes. She didn't like herself for doing that.

'Merida?'

'Yes, Zoe.'

'I did something bad to the other girl who travelled with you from Portugal.'

'What did you do?'

'I hid her shoes so that no one could find them. She had to walk home without them. And I pinched her.'

'Hm. That's not nice, Zoe. But I'm not surprised. Your mother is good and getting better but she is not perfect. When she has felt insecure and confused, scared perhaps, I am sure she has reacted badly. She has passed some of her hurt, chaos and confusion onto you.'

'What does "insecure" mean?' Zoe asked. She knew what confused meant. It usually meant that she had got something wrong. And chaos was used to refer to her bedroom.

'It means when you get little knots in your tummy that you are cannot straighten out. When your heart beats a little faster and your mouth dries up. When you are not sure whether to run to or run away. When you want to ask for help but you're afraid. When you want to hide under the bedclothes.'

Ah, yes, Zoe nodded.

'You weren't able to understand that what you were feeling was jealousy. Jealousy is when you think someone is better than you or has more than you. It comes from insecurity or not loving yourself. Jealousy is a silly emotion that only hurts you. But what is important is that you've realised that and understand why you did what you did. Talk to your mum at some point. And forgive yourself. Like yourself. You are an amazing little girl. Then talk to Ely. She's sure to know a shoemaker.'

'A shoemaker?'

'Yes, of course. You will need to get some shoes to give to Lilly.'

'Okay,' said Zoe, relieved. She was going to pull the red blanket over her head but she just drew it up to her neck instead. Vincent was still purring next to her.

She thought about kicking him but she just touched his legs with her toes. Then fell into a deep dreamless sleep.

Chapter 15 – An Invisible Message

'Wakey! Wakey!' Vincent jumped on her head. Zoe curled herself into a ball. Rain battered the campervan.

'Wakey! Wakey!'

Zoe whacked him on the arm.

'Come down, Vincent,' her mother whispered. 'Zoe is still sleeping.'

'No, I'm not,' Zoe said, opening her eyes. A slither of grey light crept in from down below. It must be morning.

'Where are we?' Vincent asked, jumping up and down like a giant flea. 'Where's the slide?'

'We are in the Faroe Islands but we are just about to take off to Iceland.'

Zoe and Vincent climbed down from the bed. Ely was sitting in the front while her mother was putting away the bed below. They were parked up by the side of an empty and very wet road.

'Morning, Zoe, morning Vincent,' Merida said.

'Morning,' Zoe and Vincent chorused.

'It's still very early but we need to get going,' Lizzie said, clipping the bed into the roof.

'What's this?' Zoe asked, picking up a piece of paper with pretty red and black houses on it.'

'I picked it up in the petrol station,' Lizzie said, going to the driver's seat. 'I thought the houses looked interesting. But we don't have time to go and see them.'

'I know them,' Vincent said.

'No, you don't,' said Zoe. 'You've never been here.' Really, Vincent was telling another fib.

'I've seen houses with grass on them. Here!' Vincent picked up his iPad and opened a page with the same houses on.

'Oh.' Zoe was impressed but she wasn't going to show it. 'Where is it then?'

Vincent didn't reply.

'It's Tóshavn, the capital of the Faroe Islands,' Ely explained, looking over at the leaflet. 'It's only a few kilometers from here.'

Zoe looked at the language but couldn't make any sense of it. She asked her mother what it was.

'Danish,' her mother said. 'The Faroe Islands are a part of Denmark. Here they speak Danish. Right, are we all ready?'

'Wait, let me look,' said Ely. She took the piece of paper from Zoe and turned it over. 'Strange.'

'Why is it strange?' Zoe stared at the glossy photo of the town. She could see nothing unusual.

'There is a drawing of a tiny shoe here. Please, has anyone got a crayon?'

Zoe opened a cupboard and took out a packet of crayons and gave Ely a green one. She wondered what Ely was going to do.

Ely started colouring. White letters appeared. They were all wiggly as if Vincent had written them. Zoe tried to read them, 'Hijalpadu okkur… What does it say? Danish is very difficult.'

'It is not Danish, it is Icelandic,' Ely gasped. 'It says, Help us. Black hole under shoehouse near port.

'Oh dear,' said Merida.

'Right, time to go,' Lizzie said, starting the engine.

'What does it mean?' Vincent said, taking the piece of paper off Ely and looking at it. Zoe snatched it off him but no matter how hard she stared at the words, they remained squiggles.

'It means,' Ely began. 'We have to go to the port. I think it's my friends, the ones I told you about, the ones who were kidnapped by Balli. They are still alive. We have to rescue them.'

Merida backfired. Loudly.

'Oh dear,' Lizzie said. 'Is it really necessary?'

'No, I'm sure they're fine,' said Merida.

'Yes, we have to,' said Ely. 'He might kill them.'

Zoe felt a current of electricity buzzing around her. She didn't know whether she was more excited, or afraid. Or, what the difference was. Her mother was agitated, even Merida appeared pensive. Ely had a determined look on her little angular face.

'I will kill the troll!' Vincent announced.

A sheep baaed outside as a flock of them crossed the road in front of them.

'Oh really, Vincent. This poor troll has been beaten, abused, lives in fear, guilt, confusion and chaos. And now you want to kill him.' Merida chuckled. 'Maybe you invite him for some tea and cake?'

Zoe looked at Ely. Ely shook her head. They all ignored Merida's suggestion.

'He is still in England. So we have a chance to rescue them,' Ely said slowly. 'Please.' She looked at Lizzie out of big dark pleading eyes.

Another sheep stopped in front of them and baaed as if to say "thank you". Zoe thought how wonderful it would be to look after sheep. She wondered if they could keep one in their garden.

'Okay, Ely, but I am responsible...' Lizzie began.

'I understand, Lizzie. I'll go and find them once we get into town.'

'But I want to go!' Vincent cried.

'No,' said Lizzie and Ely.

Lizzie turned towards Tóshavn. Merida's wheels suddenly squeaked as they turned.

'Are you okay?' Lizzie asked.

'Great,' replied Merida. 'I'm just not keen on rescue missions. I would rather be camping by the beach.'

'Me too,' said Lizzie.

'Just pretend it's a tourist trip into town. You may as well see Thor's Harbour while we're here,' Ely said.

'Who's Thor?' Zoe asked.

'Thor is the god of thunder and lightning. He protects us,' Ely explained.

'Really?' said Lizzie.

Zoe liked the idea that someone was protecting them. Outside the land and grass had been crayoned in grey. The rain had stopped but the clouds had seeped into the landscape.

'What's a god?' Vincent asked.

'Vincent!' Zoe cried. She had learned all about gods in school. Then again, Vincent was younger than her. She liked the Indian gods best, particularly the elephant god. But she knew they weren't in India now. 'You know like...' She couldn't remember the name of the elephant god. 'Like Jesus.' She knew that wasn't right.

'Jesus was a man.'

'Vincent is right. And gods are a load of old tripe,' said Merida.

Ely shook her head and tutted. Her mother let out a little laugh. Zoe could see her ready to speak but she held firmly onto both her tongue and the steering wheel. She steered around another sheep that had stopped and was staring at them.

'What's tripe?' Vincent asked.

Merida continued, 'Strictly speaking, the lining of a cow's stomach but, in this context, it means "nonsense". Gods are fantasies made up by adults to help them make sense of the world.'

'You mustn't say that, Merida,' Ely said quietly. 'You will make him angry.'

'Of course I must say that,' said Merida. 'Children should be told the truth.'

'How do you know what the truth is?'

'Thunder and lightning are explained by science, not some random act of an angry hand in the sky.'

'Well, we all believe different things,' said Lizzie calmly. 'The important thing is to respect each other's beliefs.'

'How is thunder made?' Vincent asked.

'Thunderstorms are made by moisture, unstable air and lift,' began Merida. 'Moisture in the air forms clouds and rain. Warm unstable air rises. Then the lift or the wind comes from sea breezes or mountains. High up in a thundercloud many small bits of ice bump into each other as they move around in the air. As they bump into each other they create an electric charge. Soon the whole cloud fills up with electrical charges. The positive charges form at the top of the cloud and the negative charges form at the bottom of the cloud. Since opposites attract, that causes a positive charge to build up on the ground beneath the cloud. The electrical charge on the ground concentrates around anything that sticks up, such as a mountain or a tree. The charge coming up from these points eventually connects with a charge reaching down from the clouds and that produces lightning and thunder.'

'I know that,' said Vincent. 'But how is thunder made?'

'You don't know that,' said Zoe. Really. He was right about the houses but how could he know that? Her mother didn't know that.

'I do. It's like a battery with positive and negative. And that makes electricity.'

'Very good, Vincent. Well, when a bolt of lightning travels from the cloud to the ground it actually opens up a little hole in the air, called a channel. When the light has gone the air collapses back in and creates a sound wave that we hear as thunder.'

'Wow,' said Vincent. 'I didn't know that.'

'That is true,' said Ely. 'But Thor can make one anytime he wants.'

'Wow,' said Zoe. Vincent didn't say anything for once.

Lizzie continued driving. Zoe waited. She just knew what Vincent was going to say.

'Can we make one?' he asked. 'Can we make an experiment?'

'I think we have enough to do,' Lizzie said. 'Maybe when we get home. But now we must be in Tóshavn and the sun is coming out. Look at those beautiful hills.'

Zoe looked at the grey green mountains to the left as they descended into a city of steep roofs. The red, grey, blue and cream houses reminded her of her wooden train set houses. An empty red and white bus trundled past, the first vehicle they had seen. Lizzie pulled into a car park at the harbour. Little white sailing boats swayed from side to side. Her mother looked at her phone.

'Okay. It's eight o'clock. We have three hours. Ely, do what you need to do.'

Zoe got up. Vincent followed her.

'Where're you two going?' her mother said.

'We're going with Ely.'

'Oh no you're not.'

'Please Mummy.'

'No.'

'No,' said Ely. 'I'm going to use my invisibility cloak.'

'But I want to see the houses with grass roofs,' Vincent said.

'That's fine,' Lizzie replied. 'We will go for a little walk and see the houses with grass roofs and then we'll have some breakfast. Then we're coming straight back here.'

'Okay,' Zoe said. Clever Vincent.

'Good,' said Ely. 'Put on your rain coats and take an umbrella.'

'But the sun is out!' Lizzie exclaimed.

'Yes, but it will rain. Maybe a thunderstorm.' Ely looked up at the sky.

'How do you know that?' Vincent asked.

Ely shrugged.

'She is right. Rain is forecast,' Merida said.

'How do you know?' Vincent asked.

'I've just looked at the weather report.'

Ely stopped and held up her hand for them to do the same. A huge clap of thunder slapped the air above them.

'Ah! What was that?' asked Zoe, grabbing Vincent's hand.

'Thor, of course,' said Ely. 'Come on, let's go. He just wanted to say hello to Merida.'

Merida chuckled. Zoe got her coat and Lizzie got Vincent's. The campervan door slid open and the moist air gusted around them.

'Right, I need to find a black hole under a house near the port,' Ely said. 'I'm heading over there.' She pointed to the houses with gardens on their roofs. 'Please don't be long. We might need to make a quick escape.'

'Okay,' said Lizzie. 'We won't be more than an hour.'

'Look, there's the roof made of gardens!' Zoe shouted, pointing in roughly the same direction.

'Come on then. We'll see you later, Merida. Don't go anywhere without us.'

Merida chuckled.

Lizzie locked the campervan.

'Hand please, Zoe and Vincent.'

The air smelled of earth and sea. Seagulls squawked as they rollercoasted through the tumbling winds. Zoe tried to tug her mother forward but Ely soon disappeared from view. They passed by the red houses, along the stone streets. Small groups of people also wandered around, taking photographs.

'Here's a black house,' whispered Vincent to Zoe, trying to peer in through a gap in the doors.

'Vincent, please don't climb up the doors,' Lizzie said. 'Look at those green grass roofs!'

But neither Zoe, nor Vincent were listening to Lizzie. They were both too intent on looking for Ely and her friends. They passed one black shed with its door open several inches, just enough for a child to pass through. Zoe had a strange feeling as they went by. She felt Vincent hesitate as well as they stepped over the cobbled streets. But he didn't go back.

'Look here!' said Vincent. He peered through a window on tiptoe.

Zoe tried to lift him up.

'It's full of shoes!'

'Come away, both of you. That looks like a private house.'

Zoe came away. She didn't really want to think about shoes. She wandered towards a plastic sign. Out of the corner of her eye, she spied Vincent slip back to the black shed.

'Govern… What does that say, Mummy?' Zoe asked.

'Government of the Faroe Islands,' her mother said. 'This is where the Government work.'

'But there's no one here!'

'It's still early,' her mother said. 'Let's go and get something to eat. Vincent!'

Vincent was turning a key in the door. It creaked open.

Chapter 17 – Abela and Dana

Ely ran invisibly through the streets of Thor, dodging around tourists. Occasionally she would bump into one. They would stop and look around, confused. Ely had no time for apologies or explanations. She had to find her friends and quickly. She had told Lizzie and the kids that Balli would be in England for much longer but she didn't know that for sure. What she hadn't told them was that Ely could feel things that they couldn't. And she could feel that things were not right. She was in danger. Her friends were in danger. Lizzie and the kids were in danger. Merida was in danger.

She stopped outside a shoe shop. She was close. She knew. She closed her eyes. They were there. She tried to see through walls but they were too thick. Someone bashed into her. She opened her eyes to find a large woman staring round at her. For an awful moment Ely thought that maybe her invisible cloak had come off but then she saw that the woman was looking around.

'John. Something just bashed my bottom!'

'But, honey, there's no one there. Maybe you walked into the window.'

'Of course I didn't! I'm not that stupid!'

Ely opened the door and slipped into the shop.

'Oh my! Did you see that, John. That door just opened. BY ITSELF!'

No one was in there. She went out the back where there were boxes and boxes of shoes. In the middle of the dark storeroom was a trapdoor. Ely knew that Abela and Dana were down there. If she listened carefully she could hear their whispers and the sound of the hammers shaping the shoes. At least they were still alive. She whispered to them and their incredulous cries of joy came bounding back to her. Abela came to below the trap door and told her what to do. Ely tried to lift the trapdoor but it was too heavy. She must wait for someone to come. She just hoped there would be another exit.

Chapter 18 – To the Bottom of the Sea

'Come on, Vincent,' her mother called quietly. Vincent reluctantly walked away from the now slightly ajar door of the black shed. Zoe thought she could hear the sound of a thousand distant hammers coming from somewhere below the ground. She had a strange feeling as they walked away. Vincent tried to run back but her mother caught his hand. Zoe and Vincent exchanged knowing looks.

They went to a café with a grass roof and a triangular glass house attached. Several people with small, white, fluffy dogs stood nearby. Zoe went to stroke one of them but it growled. Her mother pulled her away and they went to the black and white bar and ordered and paid for breakfast. Vincent and Zoe sat down outside in the glass house. The white dogs had gone.

As they finished their pitta bread and salad, Zoe noticed that the sky had grown darker and darker.

'Ely was right, it's going to rain,' her mother noted. 'We should get back. Almost an hour has passed anyway.'

'Look!' Vincent said, looking out of the window.

Zoe looked out of the glass and saw two children running very fast towards the harbour where Merida was parked. They must be something to do with Ely. Her mother also saw them. The first drops of heavy rain began to fall.

'That must be them! Come on!'

Zoe and Vincent jumped up and shot out of the door with Lizzie close behind them. They raced towards the car park just as the rain started thudding down. The two children had almost reached the camper. Lizzie aimed the key at Merida and unlocked the doors and the side door slid open by itself.

'Get in!' Lizzie shouted to the two children. 'It's okay! We are friends of Ely!'

The two children ahead of her leapt in without even looking back. Zoe jumped in behind Vincent, her mother last. Fear shone in their eyes. But where was Ely?

'Quick!' said Ely's voice. 'I'm here. Let's go!'

A large woman ran towards them. Three white dogs on leads joined her, barking and snapping, dragging behind them an elderly couple. Then, from round the corner, ran another man; a huge thundering giant.

'Mummy! Close the door!' Zoe shouted. 'Ely's here!' Her mother was concentrating on the buttons as if unsure which to press.

The door slammed. Ely whipped off her invisibility cloak. She was trembling and panting.

'Sit down, kids. Merida, we have an emergency.' Lizzie pressed the 'I' button and invisibility panels clamped around them.

Thunder rumbled above them and the rain fell like stones.

'I can't take off in the rain,' said Merida. 'And the invisibility shields will only last for a short time.'

'Oh.' Lizzie switched the engine and reversed, tyres screeching. 'I can't get round them without running them over! Kids, buckle up.'

'Run them over!' said Vincent, standing up to see out the window.

'Not necessary,' said Merida, dodging round them.

Zoe snapped in her seatbelt. Ely sat in the front while the other two perched in front of them. Zoe realised that one of them was not a child but a tiny woman. She must be

Ely's friend's mother. They were almost identical with their long blonde straight hair, big blue eyes and high cheekbones. Only one had lines and worn skin.

'They're still coming,' Ely cried. 'It's him! The big one. He's got a key in his hand.'

'That's Glugga,' Ely's friend replied. 'He must be working for Balli. He's the one who kept us locked up. He can see our shadow. He'll get in. He can break any lock.'

'I can't fly,' groaned Merida. 'Oh, rotten squid, you know what you must do, Lizzie. Just not too fast.'

'Right!' said Lizzie. She leaned to the side and turned the wheel round and then thrust her foot down.

The campervan drove faster and faster through the rain towards the edge of the harbour.

'Too fast!' Merida said.

'We need the speed.'

'Oh no,' Zoe murmured. Her mother was heading to the sea. She grabbed Vincent's hand. A white yacht was in front to the right. And another to the left. And another red and white fishing boat was moored up horizontally. Her mother drove faster and faster.

'Mummy!'

'Lizzie! You're going too fast.'

'No choice. We have to clear the boat. And I think there's someone behind us. Hold on everyone. Sorry Merida.' Lizzie pressed a button with a squiggly line on it.'

As they raced off the edge of the harbour there was a huffing and puffing from underneath the camper. Zoe felt the colour drain from her cheeks as they flew over the red and white fishing boat. They battered through the rain above the sea with the fishing boats and yachts tinkling around them and, for a moment, Zoe thought they were going to keep on flying. But then, bash! They hit the water.

Zoe closed her eyes, expecting to go down-down-down. But then opened them again: they were rocking about from side to side. Hooray! Zoe squeezed Vincent's hand hard. Only the sound of the rain hitting the roof. Ely and her two friends also clutched hands, fear etched on their faces, their eyes focused on the back window. All was silent for a few seconds and then an enormous SPLASH landed behind them, shuddering the campervan. Zoe screamed and held on tightly as Merida was chucked from side to side. She found herself sitting up horizontally. She could see the sea out of the window just inches from her face.

'Agh! Oh! No!'

Zoe let go of Vincent and gripped the sides of the seat. Then, just as suddenly, they tipped the right way up. And then swayed from side to side, each time less. Behind her, the red and white boat rocked violently as if a giant had shook it.

Merida bobbed about in the water like a disgruntled duck in the rain. Zoe let out a sigh of relief.

Ely and her two friends started clapping and laughing.

'Is everyone alright?' Lizzie asked, turning around. 'Where is that horrible man?'

'He fell into the water behind us,' Ely said excitedly. 'He jumped onto the other boat and tried to get onto the back of Merida but he fell. Glug-glug-glug. Down to the bottom like a stone!'

From the back window Zoe could see three people, including the couple with the dogs, looking out to sea, searching, pointing. The woman was the one dressed in a black shawl, who had chased them. But there was no sign of the big man.

Chapter 19 – The Island of the Arched Whale Bone

'That was incredible, Mummy,' said Zoe.

'Can we do it again!' said Vincent.

Merida tried to beep her displeasure but gargled instead.

'Don't be silly, Vincent,' Lizzie said, but Zoe could tell she was pleased with herself. 'Well done, Merida.'

Merida blew out bubbles from under the camper. Zoe watched the green-grey grass roofs getting further away as they drifted out to sea, away from Tórshavn. The rain still tumbled and ran down the glass window next to her. Poor Merida, Zoe thought. A line of water snaked down from the roof.

'So what happened?' Lizzie asked Ely and her friends.

Ely wobbled to the front to sit next to her mother and explained how Dana and Abela, Dana's mother, had been locked in a secret basement underneath one of the black wooden buildings: the one where Vincent had left the door open, the one where she had felt something.

'I knew you were there,' Vincent exclaimed.

'Thank you, Vincent,' Ely continued. 'Then I had to wait until the woman arrived to bring Dana and Abela breakfast so that I could get through the trap door. I crept in behind her, invisibly, of course. Dana then asked her to get some more leather for the shoes and we managed to escape – thanks to you leaving the door open.'

'And to think I nearly went back and closed it. What were you doing down there all the time?' Lizzie asked Dana and Abela.

Zoe knew the answer to that one: the hammering she had heard must have been…

'Making shoes,' Abela said. 'You know we are very good at making shoes. But we were prisoners. We were never allowed to leave. Only a couple of times the woman up there, Odna, took us out. She was nice to us. But her husband was Glugga. He would whip us if we didn't work.'

'Whip you?' said Zoe, horrified.

Merida spat up bubbles like a whale. 'Listen all,' she gurgled. 'Something far worse than whipping will happen soon. I don't know if you have noticed but we are in the sea and I am very cold and wet. According to my calculations, I cannot remain invisible for more than another ten minutes.'

'Can we take off from the water?' Lizzie asked Merida.

'I doubt it. Certainly not invisibly when it's raining,' Merida said. 'We'll have to wait until the rain stops. I will need to refuel again as well. Being a boat is very tiring, as well as drenching.'

Ely and her mother looked something up on the GPS.

'Let's go to Kongshavn,' Lizzie suggested. 'It's the nearest.'

'No, too obvious,' Ely said. She turned round and spoke to her friends. Zoe loved to listen to their beautiful voices but she didn't understand a word. She wondered if Icelandic was phonetic.

'Okay, Abela thinks Nólsoy. It's about twenty minutes ferry ride – over there – if it stops raining.' Ely pointed ahead but all they could see was the rain battering the windscreen. Merida was pitching from side to side. Zoe's tummy somersaulted. The snake of water got fatter.

'I am not a ferry. I will never get there in these waves.'

Ely said something to her friends and they held hands and started to mutter something. Zoe thought it sounded like a magic spell.

'What are you doing?'

They ignored her so Zoe took Vincent's hand and muttered something similar, 'Zei mai yo la di go rain sane whoosh.'

Zoe took a deep breath as the rain stopped and the sea calmed down. Now that was a useful thing to be able to do. If only she could remember the words she would be able to stop the rain in England.

'Do we remain invisible?' Lizzie asked Ely.

'Yes,' said Ely. 'They will be looking for us.'

'Then we need a lot more sun,' said Merida.

Abela turned her little face to the sky and said something else. Within seconds, the first finger rays of sun parted the clouds and the golden beams hit the sea.

Merida glided across the glass flat shimmering blue sea. Zoe thought she seemed a little happier but it was a long and silent crossing. Her mother looked towards a window where another line of water raced down to the purple carpet. Abela and Ely occasionally talked to each other but no one translated. Zoe watched the sea below the window. Even Vincent sat quietly playing a flying app. All she could hear was some music and the sound of crashing.

Many more than twenty minutes later, Merida's wheels touched the concrete base of a boat launch and they drove invisibly out of the sea, except for the trail of water dripping behind them, and stopped.

'What's that?' Zoe said, indicating a pointed arch which rose up and across the road that led from the sea to the village.

'They are the cheek bones of a whale,' said Abela.

'A whale?' Zoe thought she must be joking. It was huge. A van could drive underneath it. But maybe not Merida.

'Did they kill it?' Vincent asked, looking out of the window.

'Most probably,' said Ely. 'These are fishing communities. They live from the sea.'

'I don't think we'll get through those bones,' Lizzie said. 'You can't shrink yourself can you, Merida?'

'No, Lizzie. I can talk, fly and swim, if absolutely necessary. But I am not Alice.'

Abela and Dana began talking to each other.

'They seem to think we can drive through it,' Ely said. 'There must be trucks that come here.'

'I'm not risking it,' said Lizzie. 'If we get stuck in a whale bone we will cause a big scene.'

'Boats use diesel,' Dana said quietly. 'There must be diesel somewhere.'

'I can't see any pumps,' Zoe said, looking all around. Red, cream and black houses with green or grass triangular roofs dotted the harbour. Definitely no petrol station or pumps.

'I will go out and have a look around,' Ely said.

'When we open the door we are no longer invisible as the shield has to come up,' said Merida.

'I can't see anyone about,' said Lizzie.

'Over there!' said Vincent.

A man was rolling up some fishing nets.

'Hm. He is busy,' said Ely. 'I think we have no choice. If we cannot fly or drive out of the harbour, then we need to get some diesel here. Let's drive near the end of the harbour, let me out and then go back towards the whale bone arch invisibly. Do you have some money, Lizzie?'

Her mother nodded, gave Ely 100 krone, and drove Merida out of the sea. Merida's wheels squeaked as she rolled onto the concrete boat launch. Zoe had the impression she wanted to shake herself like a dog. Her mother parked so that the side door faced out to sea. Ely whipped the cloak around her, swished open the door and slipped out. Lizzie closed the door and shield behind her.

Zoe and Vincent scrambled over to sit in the front seat. Dana and Abela watched from behind. Zoe didn't want to think about what would happen if Ely didn't find any diesel.

'Okay, I'll drive towards the bones now.' Lizze drove very slowly down the pier to the entrance of the village.

The man mending the fishing nets stood up and looked around as they passed. He frowned.

Zoe looked to where Ely had headed but she could see nothing. The man was looking directly at them. He could clearly hear the engine and Merida squeaking.

'Can you not be quiet Merida?' Lizzie whispered.

'No.'

Her mother parked near to one side of the whale bone arch and cut the engine. The man shook his head and went back to his nets. They waited. The small fishing harbour was still empty.

'Look!' said Vincent, pointing to an object flying slowly towards them.

A red stick like a giant dragonfly hovered through the air. It swayed from side to side and back to front as it flew through the air about two feet from the ground. Sometimes it grew a long body, sometimes it disappeared as Ely clearly tried to hide whatever it was in her invisibility cloak. Zoe tried to think what it could be.

'It must be Ely,' Vincent said excitedly.

Zoe and Vincent squashed their faces against the window. As it came closer, Ely must have banged against the side of the van and then they saw the dragonfly becoming a watering can. The petrol cap snapped open and then glug-glug-glug. They all cheered. And off the spout went again towards one of the boats. Back and forth several times. As the red stick came towards them again, Zoe noticed that the man with the fishing net was staring at it.

'Look!' she whispered. 'He's coming towards us!'

'Okay, time to leave. We have enough fuel to take off now,' said Merida. 'Open the door and let Ely in, Lizzie.'

'But he will see us.'

'Go behind him.'

'He will hear us!'

'Switch the engine off again.'

Lizzie started the engine and drove behind him. The man turned round and dropped his nets. Just then the invisible Ely shouted and the red watering can came dancing towards him from the other direction. The man spun round and stared at it. Lizzie cut the engine. Zoe bit her lip as the red watering can landed on the ground and something appeared in its spout. He went towards it, slowly. As he bent down, Lizzie opened the door and, for five seconds, they were visible. The man took something out of the spout and stared at it in astonishment.

'Okay, I'm here. Let's go,' Ely said.

Lizzie closed the door and the invisibility shields immediately came back down.

'Quick! He's coming towards us!' said Zoe.

'Okay, we're going,' her mother said, putting Merida into flight mode.

The boxes opened on top and the blades unfolded and began to whirl. The man put his arm in front of his face as the wind from the blades rushed towards him. Merida rose up and off they turned towards north. The man looked up into the darkening sky and shook his head.

'That was close,' Ely said.

'What was in the watering can?' Zoe asked.

'100 krone. I didn't want anyone to think we'd stolen the diesel.'

'Well done. Where did you get the diesel from?' Lizzie asked.

'There was a small plastic barrel next to one of the boats. It was quite heavy so I decided to empty it into that can. I hope they don't mind.'

'Where to now? We have enough for a short journey but we still need to get more,' Lizzie said.

Ely looked up the GPS. 'Merida, can you check there's a gas station on Sørvágur?'

'Yes, there is. I should be able to make it there without falling into the sea. Just.'

'Okay, let's do it.'

Zoe felt her eyes heavy as Merida landed once again and pretended to be a normal camper. It was already dark. The days must be shorter than in Norwich as Zoe was sure they hadn't been awake for a whole day. Her mother bought petrol and more pitta sandwiches and then drove off again. Just as soon as they were on the edge of the village they munched on the sandwiches and disappeared.

'Time to sleep,' said her mother, getting up and pulling down the bed.

Zoe looked at the iPad.

'But it's only 17 o'clock!'

'Five o'clock. It's been a long day and tomorrow will be another long day. Maybe Abela will read you a story?'

'Of course,' said Abela.

Abela perched on the edge of their bed and told them a story about a puffin, called Gaia, who was picked on by the other puffins as she didn't have an orange beak. None of the other puffins wanted to be with her so she flew south and met a little boy called Pedro who lived by the sea. Together they used to fish from his boat and, at night, she would sleep in a hutch in the boy's garden with his rabbit, Rupert. But in the summer it got too hot so she said goodbye to Pedro and flew back home to the Faroe Islands. She found that much of her old colony had disappeared as the puffins had been hunted by men. So she headed north and made friends with the rabbits and they began to share nests in the rabbit burrow far away from human footsteps for all the puffins to be safe. Soon there were more and more puffins and Gaia became their most loved puffin of all.

'Next stop: Tröllaskagi,' Zoe heard Ely say. 'The Troll Peninsula.'

Chapter 20 – Zoe's Request

A pink light gently draped the camper when her mother awoke her. She felt something heavy lying on top of her: Vincent. She pushed him off, still fast asleep, and let herself down. They were parked at the side of a road. Zoe counted three cars. The houses were similar to the Faroe Islands but less colourful. These were mainly all white or grey. A high snow-peaked mountain loomed up behind the houses. Snow dusted the ground and, occasionally, a flake twirled through the air from the pale blue sky. A small church poked its spire high above the other buildings. All was quiet. There were no people. Zoe shivered.

'This is where we live,' said Ely. 'It is a small village. And that is the slide.'

She pointed to the high mountain that sat behind the village like a giant crouching.

Zoe smiled but didn't say anything. She stared at the mountain. The snow looked deep. There looked like there could be three or four slides side by side but she could not see lifts or ways of getting up there.

'Can we go?' Vincent said, jumping down from the bed.

'Yes, just as soon as it gets light,' Ely said. 'It will snow soon so it will be even better.'

'How are you going to get to the top?' Merida asked. 'I'm not sure it's a good idea to start flying. We might draw attention to ourselves.'

'No, I will arrange a Cat,' said Ely.

'A cat?' Zoe couldn't imagine a cat pulling a sledge. Even less riding on one.

'A machine, a piste basher. I will order one to bash the snow slides and then it will take us up.'

'What if Balli comes back?' Lizzie said.

'It's not possible. He's too far away. He could be away for weeks.'

'Can we go now?' Vincent started jumping up and down.

Abela and Dana stood up. Ely joined them.

'I will go and organise things,' said Ely. 'I suggest you dress up warm. And eat something. They'll be nothing on the mountain.'

'Thank you so much,' said Abela to Lizzie. 'We are extremely grateful. If there is anything we can do for you, we will.' She looked at Zoe and Vincent as she spoke.

'Thank you,' Lizzie said. 'But you must go home. You've been away for a long time.'

'Maybe the children have something to ask of you?' Merida said.

'No,' said Zoe quickly. She felt her face burn.

Dana and Abela waited.

'Ice cream?' Vincent said, hopefully.

'Yes, of course,' Abela said. 'We will bring you some. Or have some sent. We will not tell people we are back yet as news spreads quickly and we don't want the wrong people finding out.'

'Thank you!' said Vincent.

'Bye, Vincent and Zoe. Bye, Lizzie and Merida.'

The door swished open. Dana and Abela stepped out and scurried down the road, huddling in their summer clothes. Ely wrapped her cloak around her and disappeared.

Zoe sat down silent. She couldn't ask. She felt silly.

'I think you forgot something, Zoe, but it doesn't matter. It's not your fault...'

She jumped up and ran out after them. 'Wait!' The cold bit her all over.

Abela and Dana stopped and looked round.

'Please, will you do something for me?' Zoe swallowed. Her voice vibrated a little as she asked them and she found herself short of breath.

'Of course, Zoe. We were wondering when you would ask.'

Zoe smiled and ran back to the van. Her mother asked her what she was doing.

'I just wanted a little present, something special from Iceland, Mummy.'

'Zoe! That's not nice. They've just been imprisoned for a year.' Her mother paused. 'It better not be a cloak!'

That would have been good, thought Zoe, as she shook her head. 'No, Mummy, promise.'

'Oh, don't worry, Lizzie. It is nothing much and they are more than happy to fulfil Zoe's request.'

'How do you know?' Lizzie said, shaking her head.

Chapter 21 – The Cat and the Slide

Lizzie made everyone an omelette, boiled potatoes and some baked beans. Zoe sat down in front of Vincent. She folded her arms. She really wasn't hungry. Her tummy was somersaulting after talking to Abela and Dana. Her mother hovered above them with the frying pan in her hand. She slid an omelette onto Vincent's plate.

'I don't want it,' said Vincent folding his arms.

'Me neither,' said Zoe.

'Why not?' said her mother. 'I've gone to a lot of trouble to make it.'

'Yuck!' said Vincent, pushing his plate away.

'I hate potatoes,' said Zoe. 'No, Mummy, thank you. It looks disgusting.'

Zoe saw a wave of anger pass across her mother's face. She wondered if she was going to throw it at them. She'd done that before.

'Vincent,' said Merida quickly. 'What happens when I run out of diesel?'

'I don't know.'

'I don't work anymore. It means I can't go anywhere. It's the same for you. If you don't eat you run out of energy.'

'I'm never hungry.'

'Me neither,' said Zoe.

'I'm never hungry either,' said Merida. 'I never feel like I need more diesel but when you see that red light flashing we all know that I need some. I'm full now as we called in at a petrol station when you were asleep. But now I can feel a red light flashing in all of you so if you don't want to run out of fuel on the slide you had better eat everything up. You too, Lizzie. You've had a long journey. Quick. Before Ely comes back. I think, quite simply, no eat, no slide, because if one of you runs out of fuel, we're not going to be able to get you down. It will be too risky.'

'Why?' said Vincent.

'Because it is hard to carry another person down the mountain and the cold can be dangerous. Even more important is water. Drink.'

Zoe looked at the plate, picked up a fork and stabbed a potato. She wanted to go on the slide. And she didn't want to run out of fuel. She nibbled it. It wasn't as bad as it looked. And the brown bits on the omelette tasted nice. She started to gobble it up. So did Vincent. Her mother hadn't even sat down when she said, 'Finished!'

'What about your orange juice?' her mother said.

Both she and Vincent picked the glasses of juice up with both hands and gulped them down. She wiped her mouth with her hand.

'Well done,' Merida said. 'I can see you are almost full. Only Lizzie left.'

'We won!' Vincent said.

'Hm,' said Lizzie, sitting down with her omelette. 'Thank you, Merida. Sometimes, I really don't understand children.'

'Ah, they're just too excited to eat. Well done, Lizzie. You stayed in control.'

'Thanks to you.'

'Not only.'

Ely knocked on the door. 'Are we ready?'

They were.

Ely was wearing a black padded jacket, thick green trousers, a woollen hat with a large pom-pom and brown boots. She carried three extra pairs of boots, hats and gloves for them, one large and two smaller pairs. 'Here,' she said. 'Put these on. It is -1. It is not as cold as it should be but it is still cold.' She handed them out to Zoe, Vincent and her mother and picked up the three flat sleds.

'The Cat's ready,' Ely said, 'but as soon as she starts up it is possible that everyone will come out as no one has dared to go up that mountain for years. But you will get the first slide.'

'Yippee!' said Zoe, feeling her head beginning to sweat in the hat.

'I think I will stay here,' said Lizzie. 'I'm rather tired and we still have to get home.'

'Of course,' said Ely. 'I will take Zoe and Vincent.'

'Please come, Mummy,' Zoe said.

'No, honey. I need to rest. I will watch you come down, okay?'

'Okay,' said Zoe. 'Ah, I must take Milly and Chipeto!'

'Maybe just take one?' her mother suggested.

Zoe stuffed Milly inside her jacket and promised Chipeto that he would go on next time. He didn't seem bothered.

The three of them stepped outside with the snow sleds. Zoe held Vincent's hand. The mountain looked big. An enormous red snow plough with caterpillar tracks was waiting at the foot of the mountain. Behind it was an open trailer. The driver, Eric, greeted them with green twinkling eyes and wide smile, lifted them into the trailer, and told them to hold on. Zoe was glad of the gloves which were the warmest things she'd ever put on her fingers.

The Cat started towards the mountain and then began its ascent. Straight up.

Vincent started whooping. 'Look! We're almost …'

'What?' shouted Zoe. She could hardly hear.

'It's alright,' said Ely. 'Eric is experienced driver.'

Zoe looked down to the village, which was getting smaller every second. She thought it strange that everywhere was so empty. She wondered if all the people wore invisibility cloaks.

'Many people go to work in Akureyri,' explained Ely. 'And many people have left because of Balli. The rest are inside or at school.'

The Cat slid up the mountain, bashing down a path as it went. Up, up, up they climbed. Down below three people appeared at the foot of the mountain, pointing up at them. Ely waved and shouted something.

'Look!' said Vincent. 'A volcano!'

Zoe followed his gaze to a mountain shaped like an upside down ice-cream cone with the bottom bit broken off. Smoke seemed to be rising from it. But maybe it was the clouds.

'Ah, they are everywhere,' said Ely. 'That's Krafla, I think. It's supposed to be sleeping but you never know when they wake up. Or when they are woken up. They are not pleased by the melting glaciers.'

As they reached the top, snow danced through the air but Zoe could still see the blue sky behind the white flakes. Mountain tops glimmered through the clouds while, below them, flickered lakes, bare trees and strange monster-shaped rocks.

Ely threw down the sleds and jumped off the trailer. A freezing gust slapped Zoe in the face as she took the sled from Ely. They lined the sleds up along the top of the mountain. A ledge provided a starting point. From there the Cat had ploughed straight down. It was an almost vertical drop from the ledge and fell straight down the mountain to the village. It was a long long way down. Definitely the longest slide in the world. More people, now the size of playmobile characters, had gathered outside the village. Zoe took a deep breath. Surely they weren't going to go straight down there?

'Right,' Ely said. 'You sit on the sled, hold onto the plastic handles at the side and off you go. Who's going first?'

'Me!' said Vincent.

Zoe didn't say anything.

'Well done! I will go after you so any problems I will help you.'

Vincent sat down on his red sled near the edge and held onto the handles. Zoe bit her lip. She felt butterflies fluttering in her stomach.

'Ready?' Ely asked.

'Yes!'

Ely nudged Vincent off the edge and he flew down like a marble on a plastic slide. He screeched with joy. If he could do it so could she.

'Wow!' said Ely. 'Ready?'

'Yes!' she cried.

Zoe sat on her purple plastic sled and grabbed the handles. She tucked her boots into the bottom and gripped the sides. Her heart thumped loudly.

'Okay, after three: one, two, three, go!'

Zoe felt herself tip over the edge and, for a second, thought she was going to fall forever but then she was whooshing down the mountain. Down, down, down. Faster, faster, faster. She gripped the handles at the side of the sledge. The wind whipped her cheeks and took her breath away. Her mouth opened and curled up into a smile. She whooped with joy. This was amazing. This was the fastest slide ever. The sled hit a little bump in the snow and she flew into the air. She screamed. Then laughed as she landed and kept on going. Faster than she had ever been. Ever. Ahead of her, Vincent was almost at the bottom. The people were getting bigger. They were clapping and shouting. There was her mum watching her, taking photos. The sled jumped again. Zoe held on. Milly was flapping around her neck as if trying to get out of her coat. Incredible. Amazing. Fabulous. Fab. Fab. Fab. On and on she went until she came to a gentle glide just in front of Vincent.

'Again!' he shouted.

'Again!' she echoed.

Ely slid into them. She laughed. 'You enjoyed? Was it worth it?'

'Yes!' They both cried.

Lizzie appeared and hugged them both.

'It was fantastic, Mummy. We're going again! Only take Milly please. She tried to jump out of my coat.'

'Okay, honey.' Her mother took Milly. 'But we only have a couple of hours. I will go and get some diesel. And then we have to get going. We have a long way back home.'

Zoe wasn't listening. Her eyes were focused on the slide.

'Come on then!' Ely said. 'You have time for two more!' She said something to the crowd and they cheered. Some of them came forward, others dispersed.

'Where are they going?' Zoe asked.

'To get their sleds,' Ely said triumphantly.

117

Chapter 22 – The Troll's Mountain

Zoe and Vincent ran to the Cat and climbed up into the trailer. Other children were running towards them, dragging their sleds behind, smiling at them, giving them the thumbs-up. Even some adults. Soon the trailer was full and everyone was chatting away. Zoe didn't understand much of what they were saying, but she understood that they were all very happy. Several of them smiled at her and patted her on the arm. Zoe felt a big smile ripple through her. She was here, going up a mountain in Iceland about to go down the best slide in the world. Perfect.

She went first this time. Her heart still flapped like a caged bird but now she was grinning. As she tipped over the edge she cried out to the world – yippeeeee! Then screamed as she hit a little bump and flew into the air, landed and continued racing down. Ahhhhh! Wow, wow, wow. Look at me! Merida would be impressed. Zoe hoped she was watching. Now she could hear Vincent screaming as he set off. As she flew down she couldn't help but wonder about the blue shimmering slide in Norwich and Lilly. Maybe Zoe would be able to make the slide shimmer one day.

She slowed down and came to a stop and waited for Vincent to crash into her. A woman came with ice-creams and gave them to her and Vincent. 'From Abela,' she said. Zoe thanked her and took off her glove to hold the cone. She looked for her mother to ask her if it was okay but she wasn't there so Zoe began to eat it. It was the creamiest and sweetest ice-cream she had ever tasted. Both she and Vincent gobbled them up in seconds. They didn't bother waiting for Ely to come down and ran to Eric and the trailer which was coming down the mountain again. An even larger group of people were waiting, some with skis, others with sleds. Eric, the driver, smiled and joked as he helped everyone on. She still couldn't see her mum. They got on again. Now, the trailer was full of people with skis as well as sleds. At the top Ely controlled the sled run, making sure that the person in front was at least halfway down the mountain before the next person set off. Other parts of the mountain were soon covered with skiers and people with sleds preferring a slower journey down the mountain.

Everyone was so busy having fun that no one seemed to notice a black snowmobile going up the mountain. Zoe certainly didn't. It was only when she and Vincent reached the bottom and saw that everyone was shouting, not in fun but in panic, and skiing or sledding down as quickly as possible, did she look up and see the black snow mobile crossing over the ridge of the mountain. Her smile shrank away.

'Look!' she said.

'Balli!' someone shouted to them, holding their skis and pointing in the direction of the mountain. 'You must go.'

'But where is Ely?' she asked.

'Really, it is better to go,' said the woman who had brought them the ice-cream.

The black snow mobile disappeared over the ridge to the other side of the mountain. At that moment, the cloud came down and the snow fell out in big fat lumps.

'Where's Mummy?' said Zoe, panicked. She looked around at the small crowd around her but she wasn't there. 'Where is she, Vincent?'

'I don't know,' little Vincent said, looking around. 'And Ely? Where is she?'

119

'Do you want to come and wait at our house?' a young woman asked. 'We live over there.'

Zoe shook her head. She must wait where her mummy would find them. 'Where did Mummy say she was going?'

Vincent shook his head. Neither of them had been listening.

'How did Balli get back so quickly?' Zoe asked.

Everyone shrugged and shrank away. The snow was falling heavily now.

Eric arrived in the Cat. He had his mobile phone in his hand. He began talking to the few remaining people there. He kept pointing to the mountain.

'Balli take Ely. Come on, Zoe and Vincent. Come, sit with me in the cabin and we wait for your mother. Will come soon I think.'

Zoe and Vincent climbed up. The heat melted the snow on them in seconds and puddles gathered around their feet.

'Are we going after Ely?' Vincent said.

'We cannot,' said Eric. 'I call the police and mountain rescue but Balli's snow mobile is so fast, his tracks are already covered by snow.'

'But what about Ely? Will she be all right?' Zoe asked.

'She can look after herself,' said Eric, but his voice did not sound sure.

'Look! Is that Mummy? Yes! She's looking for us.' Zoe waved out of the window, a wave of happiness crashing over her.

'That is good,' said Eric. He started the Cat and crunched towards her.

Her mother looked puzzled when she saw them in the Cat. They stopped alongside her and Zoe jumped out and fell into her arms. Her mother hugged her tightly. And then pulled Vincent towards her as well.

'What happened?'

Eric told her mother what had happened.

'But how did he get here so quickly?'

Eric shook his head.

'He must have flied,' said Vincent solemnly.

'It's the only way,' said Eric. 'Ely will be okay. As soon as the snow stops we look for her.'

'Okay,' said her mother. 'Then it is time for us to go.'

Eric nodded. 'I am sorry Balli spoils the day. He always does that.'

'That's okay,' said Lizzie. 'We brought Ely back and the kids went on the slide. I'm sorry for you that you have to live with such a horrible man.'

'He is not a man,' Eric muttered. He bent down to shake hands with Lizzie and waved goodbye to Zoe and Vincent, started up the Cat and beep-beeped away, an orange flashing light on top.

'Come on, quick, back to Merida,' her mother said taking hold of both their gloved hands. 'I can't see her in this snow.'

'Where were you?' Zoe moaned.

'I went to get diesel. Remember?'

Zoe didn't. The snow covered them entirely by the time they got back to the camper. They jumped into Merida and the door swished behind them.

'Merida, Merida…' Vincent began as Lizzie tugged off his gloves and coat.

Zoe tried to get her boots off. Her feet were still cosy and dry. If they went now she wouldn't see Abela again.

'Hello Vincent and Zoe, did you enjoy the slide?'

'Yes, but Balli took Ely and he has disappeared on a snow bike. She's gone.'

'What?'

They told Merida all they knew. She was silent.

'So, are we ready to go home?' said her mother, hanging up the wet clothes in the toilet.

No one replied.

Chapter 23 – The Snatch

Within seconds of Balli appearing on top of the mountain he had grabbed Ely from behind, tied her to his snow mobile and was thundering north, away from the slide and the village. Ely's hands were bound behind her back so she had to grip the snowmobile with her legs to stop herself from falling off. She was furious for getting caught. Why hadn't she known? Why hadn't she felt his presence?

She had felt nothing but happiness. Happy that she was home, happy that her new friends were enjoying themselves, happy that her old friends were safe. Happy that Balli was gone. The ice whipped her face. She didn't even have her invisibility cloak with her. How had he got back from England? Would he never let them live in peace? She remembered Merida's words: *Can you imagine what a horrible childhood he must have had? To want to*

hurt others he must have been so badly hurt. Each generation is recycling the same rubbish childhoods. Each generation of trolls is learning anger, and how to hate and hurt. It's just not necessary.

'Balli!' she shouted through the wind. 'Can we talk?'

The roar of the snowmobile almost blocked out the troll's roar.

He only stopped when he reached a pine forest but only for a minute. Then he raced up a steep track and cut the engine.

He grabbed Ely.

'You want to talk?' He shook her like a little doll.

'Balli! Let me go! I want to say sorry.'

'Sorry! You rob me of my mountain. It is all I have left! You are a thief. And like a thief I will lock you up. This time where no one will find you. And you cannot disappear on me this time.'

'Please, Balli. No one was ever going to steal the mountain. We wanted to do business.'

Balli spat a big glob of yellow that fizzled in the snow.

'BUSINESS! You call plans to put up a gondola on MY MOUNTAIN without permission BUSINESS?

'But we were trying to ask you!' Ely cried out desperately.

'And I said NO! IT IS MY MOUNTAIN.'

Ely could feel the ground beneath her feet shaking.

'But it would be good for the whole community…' Her words blew away with the snow.

'What do I care about your community?' He roared. 'All my life I have had to fight for my mountain. I am NOT MOVING. And neither are you.'

He picked her up and put her under his arm. She tried to wriggle free but he held her tight. Her only defense was reason. But how could she reason with him?

'Balli, I'm sorry you weren't treated very well...' She hesitated at her words.

He stopped, screamed, held her upside down and put a stinking sock in her mouth and a balaclava over her face. She could no longer speak or see where he was taking her. Maybe that hadn't been the right thing to say.

'We can't really leave Ely in the hands of Balli,' said Merida.

'Merida, I am not risking the lives of the children,' said Lizzie, sitting down in the driver's seat.

'But we must help her!' said Vincent. 'He will turn her into stone!'

'Don't be silly, Vincent. That is not possible,' said Merida. 'But we should help her. She's our friend. And friends help each other.'

'But Merida. We brought her back here. We did help her. I have responsibilities too. You can't fly in the snow. It's too dangerous.'

Merida fell silent again. 'You are also right, Lizzie.'

'Thank you.'

Vincent let out a cry like an injured animal, bashing the metal seatbelt as the side of his booster chair. Zoe's heart hung heavy in her chest as she clicked in her seatbelt.

'Zoe, can you help Vincent please?' her mother asked.

'No,' she said.

'Zoe! Do what I ask please.'

'NO!' she screamed. 'I don't want to!'

'Zoe, what is the matter with you!'

'Zoe, it's okay,' Merida said calmly. 'You've done really well. Maybe we can get some shoes on the way.'

'What are you on about!' her mother shouted. 'What shoes?'

'Nothing,' Zoe said, but helped Vincent.

'Right? Are we ready now?'

No one replied. Lizzie started the engine. Vincent opened his iPad and tapped in the code. Zoe stared out of the window. It was still snowing.

Lizzie pulled off. 'I reckon we drive to the east of the island and take off. According to my phone it is not snowing there.'

No one said anything.

They drove slowly in silence. Lizzie had to use the satnav to find the buried road. Zoe's tummy churned. She doubted she would ever see Abela and Dana again. Or Ely. It was the best slide ever. Followed by the worst end. How easy it was for things to go so wrong.

Merida crunched through the snow for what seemed like hours.

'I'm feeling heavy,' said Merida, finally breaking the silence. 'And it's not because of a rock. It's because of your thoughts. You are not feeling good. And when you don't feel good, I feel like I have three rocks on board. Now what shall we do?'

'We need to find Ely,' said Vincent, without looking up from his iPad.

'We can't,' Lizzie said firmly, clutching the steering wheel. 'We're going home. We've done what we came to do. Ely would not want us to risk our lives.'

'That is your head saying that, Lizzie. We know that we shouldn't look for Ely because it is dangerous. But now examine your feelings. What do you feel?'

'That we should go home,' said Lizzie.

'If that is how you feel, then why am I so heavy?'

'You're imagining it. You're a computer, for goodness sake.'

Merida didn't reply.

'Mummy, Merida is right,' Zoe said. 'We need to find Ely.'

'Yes,' said Vincent. 'You know.'

Lizzie didn't reply. She kept her eyes on the road ahead.

'Lizzie, Zoe and Vincent feel it. It is harder for you as you are an adult and you are blocking your feelings. It is normal. It is what you have learned. But get rid of that rubbish. Get back to the truth. Remember you are all remarkable. You have come on this fantastic journey. You helped someone on the way. Incredible. Now, as much as I would like to return to the warm beaches of Portugal, what do you feel you should do?'

'Help Ely,' Lizzie said quietly.

'Hooray!' shouted Zoe and Vincent.

And, as if by magic, Merida almost took off without the help of the rotor blades.

'Yes,' said Merida. 'That's better. You see, we can feel when we make the right decision. I feel so much lighter.'

'Slow down! Okay, but now what do we do?'

'Keep going. We have to get out of this snow,' Merida said.

The snow stopped falling and, after travelling a few more kilometres, Lizzie pulled over. Patches of blue swam above them. Strange rocks, dressed in white, watched them from the sides of the road.

'Okay, so the Troll peninsular is a little behind us but we could take off from here and head back. He went into the mountains, didn't he?'

'Yes, up there!' Zoe pointed to the mountains behind them to the right. But they were still covered in cloud.

'According to the weather app it is still snowing in the mountains,' Merida said. 'We need to wait a while.'

'Okay, then kids do you want to go and play for ten minutes?'

Zoe and Vincent pulled on their boots and put on their hats, coats and gloves and went outside. Zoe scooped some snow into her hand, moulded it into a ball and... SPLAT! Something hit her in the face. 'Vincent!' she shouted. But as she went to throw it, she noticed that he hadn't even bent down to collect snow. He was staring at one of the rocks.

'What?'

She looked around. The rocks seemed to be laughing at her. She threw the snowball at one of the rocks. At that same moment another one landed splat in her face.

'It moved!' shouted Vincent. A snowball landed on his head.

Her mother came out and scanned the sky. A snowball landed on her shoulder. 'Hey!' She sat down on one of the rocks and slid off.

'The rocks are moving,' said Vincent. 'Quick! They are the trolls.'

'Don't be silly,' said Lizzie, brushing the snow off her bottom. 'But maybe we should go. Look at that blue sky. It's clearing.'

For once, Zoe didn't need telling ten times and jumped into the camper. Vincent was right.

Chapter 25 – Balli

'Sit at the front,' Lizzie told Zoe and Vincent. 'We're going to have to look very carefully.'

Liz pressed the 'I' button. The invisibility shields clamped around them, the rotary blades unfolded from the roof of the camper, and Lizzie started the helicopter engine. WAP-WAP-WAP-WAP-WAP-WAP-WAP-WAP.

'We're off,' Merida said, as they lifted up into the blue sky and headed up towards the pyramid mountain behind them.

Zoe smiled to herself. However much chewing gum Sheena stuck in her hair she would never forget flying over mountains and sea in Merida.

'Keep your eyes peeled,' Lizzie said. 'I'll look to the left, you look to the right, Zoe, and Vincent, look in front We are looking for snow mobile tracks.'

The glittering white snow below was almost blinding in the sunlight. As they flew closer to the pyramid mountain, Zoe could see no tracks, no trees, no rocks. Only snow and water. In the valleys little streams were beginning to flow. Merida went closer as they approached the top of the pyramid and then over to the other side where mountain after mountain came into view, all nestled together.

'We will never find them,' said Lizzie.

'Look!' said Vincent. 'What's that? A track!'

Sure enough down one side of the mountain there looked like a sled track.

'No,' said Lizzie. 'That's where snow has fallen.'

Come on, Zoe said to herself, please, we need to find them.

They flew down into a valley. Trees shivered in the sun, shaking off some of the snow. Zoe still could not see any tracks.

'He must have taken her either to a cave or a mountain hut,' said Merida.

'Unless they left the mountains?' Lizzie said.

'They wouldn't have had time,' said Merida. 'And it has been snowing, remember. They couldn't have got that far. Over to the left is the mountain where the slide is, about three mountains away.'

'There!' said Zoe. Two thin lines ran faintly down the next mountain. That was the snowmobile, surely.

'Yes!' said Lizzie. 'Well done. Now we just have to follow them down.'

'No,' said Vincent. 'Up. Look, they go up.' He pointed in front. He was right. The lines ran along the side of a mountain, then down towards a valley and disappeared into some pine trees.

'I can't land in there,' Merida said. 'I will fly around and see if we can see if there are any more tracks.'

Zoe felt her heart thumping hard as she realised that Ely and Balli could be somewhere in those pine trees. Merida hovered at the edge of the trees. Ely must be able to hear them.

'Can you see anything?' Lizzie asked.

No one replied.

'Look!' said Zoe. 'They must be looking for Ely!' She pointed to the small helicopter that wapped into view through the mountains.

'Okay,' said Lizzie. 'Then maybe we can go…'

'No Mummy, we need to make sure Ely is safe,' said Zoe.

'We need to get out of the way,' said Merida. 'It might crash into us.'

'Let us out,' said Vincent. 'Then we can wave to them.'

'Too dangerous, but throw a torch out of the door so they will see the tracks,' Lizzie said.

Vincent scrambled into the back and found the torch, switched it on. Lizzie opened the door for a moment while Vincent dropped it out. Merida spun round so they could see where it landed near the edge of the pine trees. The beam glared up from the snow.

'Perfect,' said Lizzie.

The helicopter swung towards the light as Merida veered away. Merida followed the tracks back up the mountain and landed near the top. Down below four people emerged from the helicopter and headed into the pine trees to look for the torch.

Within seconds, a snowmobile revved up and shot out of the trees straight towards them.

'It's him!' Zoe gasped.

'Go visible, Lizzie,' said Merida.

'Oh dear,' said Lizzie, tapping the 'I' button so the invisibility panels lifted.

The snowmobile saw them and slowed down. Zoe held her breath. It stopped. Balli got off and marched towards them. He was small, stocky, slightly bowlegged. He wore black boots, thick ski trousers and a balaclava. There was no sign of Ely. He started roaring at them. None of them could understand a single syllable.

'Ask him if he'd like a cup of tea, Lizzie.'

'Don't be ridiculous!'

Before anyone could stop him, Vincent jumped up and opened the door.

'Hello!' he called. 'Would you like a cup of tea?'

Balli stopped in his tracks. He growled something, presumably in Icelandic.

'Are you Balli?' Zoe asked, aware of her mother standing behind her, ready to close the door at any moment.

'Ask him to come in,' said Merida.

'Don't be...'

'Would you like to come in?' said Vincent.

Zoe thought Vincent very brave and, possibly, very stupid. Balli did not look friendly. He took a couple of steps towards them and then snatched off his balaclava. His face was sunburnt and pitted like an old stone. He roared at them again.

'I'm sorry we don't speak Icelandic,' said Lizzie.

'What you want here? Go away. Back to your country. You won't find her,' he growled. His English sounded as if he was crunching stones.

'Oh, do you know where she is?' Lizzie said, shifting Zoe behind her. Her mother's fingers shook.

Balli came closer. He snatched Lizzie by the arm and pulled her out of the camper. He twisted her arm behind her back. Zoe gasped. He spat out a green glob that burned the snow.

He grunted. 'Why you here?'

'Ouch, please. We just wanted to say goodbye to Ely.'

'Leave her alone!' Zoe shouted. He was hurting her mother. 'Please!'

'Shut it. How you get here?'

'Merida.'

'Who is Merida? What is this strange energy?'

'That's me,' Merida said. Merida spoke in Icelandic to Balli. His mouth opened as wide as a hippo's. Inside were two rotten teeth.

'Who is talking? Tell me!'

'Merida!'

Just at that moment there were several shouts from the forest. Balli pushed Lizzie into the camper in front of him. Zoe stepped back almost into the toilet. His eyes met hers. They were like green moss. She felt herself shrink. This was not a good idea. He shoved her mother in her direction and swept Vincent out of the way with one brush of his stocky right arm as he took two strides to the driver's seat. Vincent fell to the floor. Zoe tried to hold onto her mother but she rushed to pick him up. He didn't cry.

'I'm so sorry, Balli. We won't hurt you,' Merida said, before speaking in Icelandic again.

'Who are you?' Balli growled. 'How do you make invisible? And how you speak Icelandic?'

'My Icelandic is a bit rusty, I'm afraid. Press the 'I' in front of you. Show him, Lizzie,' said Merida calmly. 'Sit down Zoe and Vincent.'

Her mother showed him. Zoe and Vincent sat down in their seats. Zoe's heart thumped. The panels clamped around them. She wished Vincent hadn't invited him in. That was a massive mistake.

'I can feel your anger and pain,' said Merida.

'What do you know of anger and pain!' Balli shouted, thumping the steering wheel. 'They try to steal my MOUNTAIN!'

'Ouch. I understand...'

'No you cannot understand.' He got up and looked around for the speaker. 'All my life I have had to fight for what is MINE.'

'It's hard. It's hard,' said Merida in her soothing voice. 'Of course, the mountain is yours. Everyone must understand that. Ely most of all. But the pain and anger is beyond that, Balli. You know nearly all adults, Ely, Lizzie, yourself, carry around a certain amount of pain, conflict and confusion from childhood. It was passed on to all of you by your parents. But it is not the parents' fault either. They were also passed on a lot of confusion and conflict. Can you imagine how your mother was treated? Your father? We grow up not knowing why they have done the things they have done. And so we become angry without really knowing why.'

'How do you know what my mother did?' Balli stood up and looked around for the source of the voice. 'You don't know anything about me. Who are you?'

'I know because it is the same for everyone but some more than others. But it is not your fault...'

Balli stood with his face to the door. He let out a small cry like a hurt animal.

'Where is Ely?' whispered Zoe. 'Please tell us. We want to say goodbye.'

'Donkey stone,' he spat. Then he leant against the button to open the door and stepped out into the snow. For a moment they were all visible. Lizzie quickly closed the door and pressed the 'I' button. Not a moment too soon. Shouts came from below. Someone had spotted him. Balli was smashing his way through the snow to his snowmobile. Seconds later, he jumped on, revved the engine and roared away down the mountain.

Chapter 26 – The Laughing Donkey

Zoe jumped up and hugged her mummy. Her mother's arms embraced her and she kissed her head and smoothed away her hair.

'Well,' said Lizzie, breathing out deeply. 'That was close. I'm not sure that was clever, Merida. He could have turned nasty. Are you okay, Vincent?'

'I'm fine. That didn't hurt at all.'

'You were very brave, Lizzie and Vincent. All of you. You're right. He has a lot of anger. And angry people are dangerous. Sorry. I need more time with him.'

'Well, good luck with that. Please don't include us. You did well, Zoe. At least we have a clue. Donkey stone?'

The helicopter thwacked and came towards them.

'I hope it doesn't land on us,' said Vincent.

No one answered. They all watched out of the window and breathed a sigh of relief as it headed down the mountain after the snowmobile.

'Come on!' said Vincent. 'Let's see if we can find a donkey stone. It must be in the pine trees.'

Zoe's legs felt a little shaky. She took her mother's hand and held it tightly.

'I'm not sure, Vincent,' said Lizzie. 'If the mountain rescue team and police couldn't find her, I'm not sure we will.'

'But we have a clue!'

'Vincent's right,' Merida said. 'But, somehow I don't think she's in the pine trees. For a start there are no stones.'

'Let's look,' Vincent insisted.

Zoe, Vincent and her mother wrapped up warm. Zoe and Vincent jumped outside. The air was full of white ice dust.

The sun was bright but cold. Her mother, for some reason, was filling her rucksack with a packet of chocolate digestive biscuits, some salt and vinegar crisps, a bottle of water and, at the last minute, a white loaf of bread.

'Come on!' said Zoe impatiently. She overheard Merida asking her mother to leave her on 'ME', so she could stay invisible.

Lizzie closed and locked the door from the outside with the remote key. Then she stamped out a line in front of the door so they would know where Merida was. Zoe crunched downhill towards the trees. The helicopter was out of sight but they could still hear its thwacking in the distance. Vincent ploughed on ahead. He started to call, 'Ely!' Zoe joined in. They reached the pine trees. There were no rocks, only squashed snow where boots had crunched through the trees.

'She's not here,' said Lizzie. 'I think we should go back.'

At the other side of the pine trees rose a mountain side where no snow had stuck. Stones froze to the rock but, again, there were no donkeys. Elsewhere white snow rolled up and down like a thick layer of icing.

'There!' said Vincent, pointing up towards the rocky part of the mountain.

'Where?' asked Lizzie.

Zoe couldn't see anything other than a few rocks.

'There!' said Vincent, running towards the mountain. 'There, there, there! The donkey rock!'

Zoe still couldn't see it.

'Come on,' said Vincent. Zoe and her mum followed. Vincent started scrambling up the loose rock face.

'Careful,' warned Lizzie, following him. 'Some of the stones are loose.'

Zoe also followed, slowly. She didn't really want to climb up there.

'Vincent, I'm not sure we should go up there. It doesn't look safe.'

Zoe stopped. And as she looked she saw it! A donkey face in the rock. Two long ears pointed slightly to the left. Below them, a long face, an eye and an open mouth as if laughing. A ledge drew a ragged line underneath it.

'There it is! There it is!' She, too, started jumping up and down.

'Calm down, Zoe. Where is it?'

Zoe described it for her mother until she, too, could see it.

'Okay, then it's worth a try.'

They climbed up the cliff face. The stone was ice cold and slippery. Almost at the top, Vincent fell and slipped all the way back down.

'Are you okay?' her mother called.

Vincent stood up and immediately began climbing again.

'I'm sorry, Vincent, I can't get you.'

Zoe and her mother were nearly there but the last bit was the steepest.

'Use your hands,' her mother suggested.

Zoe crouched down and inched her way up. She put her knee on the ledge and stood up. Her mother was behind her and Vincent was catching them up. Zoe called, 'Ely!' They listened. No answer. Zoe felt the rock but it was just rock.

Her mother felt around. 'There's no opening.' Her mother shouted down to Vincent: 'Stay there, there's nothing here.'

Vincent ignored her and kept on climbing. He was nearly there. Lizzie helped him up the last bit.

'Ely!' he screeched. Even Zoe had to cover her ears. The sound reverberated around the mountains.

But then they heard a muffled cry of someone a long way away.

'She's in there! She's down below,' Zoe shouted. 'Ely! We are coming!'

Vincent jumped up and down. The stone beneath him wobbled just a fraction.

'Look! Beneath our feet. The stone moves!'

Lizzie bent down. 'Get off, Vincent, please.' Vincent hopped off. Lizzie put both hands onto the stone and tried to lift it but it was stuck.

'Try turning it like a wheel,' Zoe said.

Her mother, for once, did as she asked and the stone slowly turned revealing a hole about the size of her Snakes and Ladders board. And very dark.

'I can't get in there,' said her mother. 'And I'm not letting you two go down.'

But Vincent had already dropped himself in. 'I need a torch,' he said.

'I don't have a torch anymore but here's my phone,' said Lizzie, rummaging around her rucksack. 'I thought I picked up some matches but I can't find them. The phone light is the best.'

Vincent disappeared into the hole. He shone the light around him. 'The other stone moves, Lizzie.'

Her mother stepped into the hole and shifted the other stone to make the entrance bigger. Zoe followed. It was dark, damp and very cold.

'It's a tunnel,' Vincent called from ahead. His voice echoed.

'It's very tight,' Lizzie said on her hands and knees. 'I don't think I can go far.'

'Vincent... cent... cent! Lizzie... zie... zie...! Zo...
ee...ee!' Ely's voice was getting closer.

'We're coming... ing... ing!' shouted Vincent. He shone
the torch along the tunnel. 'There's a door... or... or!'

Zoe crouched behind her mother. She couldn't get past
her. Behind her, light still filtered in from the mountains.
What if Balli came back and shut them in? He was being
chased. He knew the area. He knew where he would find
them.

'Mummy?'

'Yes, honey?'

'I'm behind a door... or... or!' Ely shouted.

'It's here... ere... ere!' Vincent shouted.

'We're nearly there, Zoe...ee...ee,' her mother said.

'What if Balli comes here, Mummy...me,' Zoe
whispered.

'Let's just hope he doesn't. I'm sure they would have
caught him by now...ow.'

They reached some stones. Her mother immediately
started to move the stones but there was no room for them.
'We need to roll them back along the tunnel.'

The three of them busily shifted the stones until they
came to a large piece of wood.

'Push it, Ely. It should fall,' Vincent called.

The wood crashed down in front of them and there she
was.

'Come on. Quick!' Ely swept past them and down the
tunnel. Zoe, Vincent and her mother followed her.

Zoe felt her body tremble as she scrambled back along
the dark tunnel. Vincent was in front, her mother behind,
the light from her phone flashing up onto the walls of the
tunnel. Please, please, be open, she muttered to herself. She
could see a square of daylight. Her hands shook as she

climbed out. But they had made it into the bright sunshine, under the sparkling blue sky. And no sign of Balli. She slowly let out the dark, damp breath from the cave. Ely hugged them all. Despite her thermal ski clothes she looked pale and cold and her dark silky hair was matted and dull.

'I can't believe you found me,' she cried. A small tear ran down her cheek. 'Thank you, thank you. But let's go before he comes back.'

'The mountain rescue team have gone after him,' said Lizzie.

'I doubt they'll catch him. He'll just turn to stone and roll away.'

Zoe gasped some icy air. Could he really do that?

'Where's Merida?' Ely said, looking around.

'She's up there!' Zoe said.

'I can't see her,' Ely said, looking worried.

'She's on invisible mode,' Lizzie explained.

'Clever,' said Ely.

They passed the pine trees and climbed up to where Merida was parked. Zoe could see the line that her mother had made in the snow. There were also four tyre tracks in the snow. Lizzie went to open the door but she could not find it. Vincent walked into where Merida had been. Nothing. Merida had gone.

Chapter 27 – Under the Northern Lights

Her mother's face crumpled. 'I don't believe it. It's not possible. I have the key!'

They stood there. No one moved as Lizzie hunted in her pockets for the key.

'Here!' she cried, showing the key to the others.

'Is there another one?' Ely asked.

'Not,' said Lizzie, 'that I know of.'

'How did he know Merida was here?' Ely asked quietly.

'He was here. Merida invited him in,' said Zoe.

'What?!'

Lizzie explained what had happened. Ely shook her head. 'You're very lucky he let you go.'

'Maybe Merida influenced him.'

'Then why isn't Merida here? He's stolen your campervan. I doubt you'll ever see her again.'

Zoe felt tears prick her eyes. Never see Merida again? That would be terrible.

'Don't worry,' said Lizzie, taking her hat off. Her red hair was flat against her head. 'Merida can look after herself.'

'Can she fly on her own?' Ely said.

'No,' said Lizzie, hesitantly. 'I don't think so.'

Ely shrugged. 'But if he came on his snowmobile and took Merida then his snowmobile must be somewhere here.'

'Look!' said Vincent.

Snowmobile tracks led down the mountain.

'Let's follow them!'

'No, said Ely. 'Better to stay here. We don't how far it is. It would be very easy to freeze to death. At least this is where the rescue team were. They will come back. They will see us here.'

'But what are we going to do?' asked Zoe.

'Don't worry, Zoe. We'll call someone.' Lizzie put her hat back on and pulled out her phone but there was no battery charge. 'Oh no.' Zoe could hear the tears in her voice. 'I must have left the torch on.'

'Oh,' said Ely. 'Don't worry, they will find us.'

'You mean we will have to stay the night here in the snow?' Zoe felt very cold.

'Hopefully not,' Ely said.

'What if Balli comes?' Zoe said.

Zoe waited for her mother or Ely to say something comforting. Neither did. But her mother rummaged in her bag and pulled out some bread and crisps. She made everyone a crisp sandwich.

'Thank goodness we have some food,' Ely said. 'Thank you, Lizzie.'

'You're welcome. It was actually Merida's idea.'

They waited. And waited. The sun began to slide behind a mountain. The sky turned pink. No one came. They ate a little bit of snow for dessert.

'Let's make a fire,' Vincent said.

'It's too cold,' said Lizzie. 'The fire would never catch.'

'It might,' said Ely. 'If we have some matches.'

'We don't. I looked earlier.'

Lizzie took off her glove and pulled out the phone from her pocket, checking it hadn't come back to life. 'Ah, what's this? I have the box of matches! I did pick them up.'

'Then we can make a fire!' said Ely. 'Vincent, come with me. Zoe, you stay here with Lizzie in case the helicopter flies in. You never know. And keep moving. The temperature will really fall now.'

Ely and Vincent went back to the pine trees.

'What if they don't come, Mummy?' Zoe whispered. Her teeth started chattering. They might freeze to death. She remembered the story of the little matchstick girl who had used all the matches she had meant to sell in trying to keep herself warm. In the morning she was dead.

'They will, darling, they will. They know Ely is missing. They will continue searching. The sky is clear. Helicopters fly at night.'

Her words sounded convincing, her voice less so. Zoe was hungry. She dabbed her glove into the snow and stuffed some into her mouth.

'Here, have some more bread, Zoe.' Her mother handed her a slice. 'A snow sandwich!'

'Hey! Why don't we write in the snow!' Zoe said, chewing the bread. 'Then if someone flies above they will see it!'

'Excellent idea,' said her mother.

Zoe began to drag her heel through the snow several times to make one vertical line. Her mother did the same. Zoe then joined them up formed an 'H'.

'You know, I've been thinking, Zoe,' her mother said, beginning on the 'E'. 'I'm sorry if I've not been a perfect mummy. As Merida says, I learned a lot of not good things from my parents that I've realised I've passed on to you. Blaming others, criticising, being negative, thinking that other people have it all good... These are all things that I've learned. By the time you get to my age it's very difficult to reprogram. But I will try. And I want you to know that I love you more than the ...' She looked up into the darkening sky, '... the universe. More than everything. I wanted you so much. You know I couldn't have children. I waited a long time until I finally got you.'

Zoe listened. She knew that. But it warmed her to hear the words. She drew the 'L'. That was an easy one.

'Mummy, I hid her shoes.'

'Sorry, darling?' Her mother stopped writing.

'I hid her shoes in the sand.'

Her mother did not say anything but Zoe could hear her mind sifting through memories.

'The girl in the park?'

'Yes,' said Zoe. She stepped back and waited for her mother to explode.

'Okay,' her mother said slowly. 'Why?'

Zoe shrugged. 'I don't know. I wanted to go down the slide like she did.'

'Oh, Zoe. I wish I'd known.'

'Merida said I should ask Abela to make some new shoes. So I did.'

'Abela?'

'Yes, so I could take them back to her.' Zoe folded her arms and closed her mouth.

'Ah.' Deep white breath poured out of her mother's mouth. She began the 'P'. 'You are trying to put it right. Well done. That's a good thing to do.' She paused. 'I'm not sure we'll ever see those children again, honey. But we can try. When we get home. Look!'

Down below a thin trail of smoke came up from the trees.

'They've lit a fire!' said Zoe. She unclamped herself.

'Wait, let's finish the letters.' Her mother rounded the face of the 'P' with the toe of her boot. 'And, Zoe, thank you for telling me. That was a brave thing to do.' Her mother gave her a big bear hug and a freezing cold kiss on her cheek.

'Brrr!' Zoe said. But she was glowing inside.

146

She looked down at the four letters: HELP. Then she floated down to the pine trees, lighter than a leaf. She had told her mother. Her mother had not told her off. They would get the shoes. She would find the girl. And she would never do anything like that again. She would be the one to fly down slides. And, if she didn't, she could always remember the best slide in the world. All was wonderful. Well, except for the cold, Merida having disappeared and being lost on a freezing mountain with a nasty troll loose.

Zoe and her mother joined Ely and Vincent who were squatting in front of the fire warming their faces. The last bit of light had gone from the sky. Now it was the stars' turn. They flickered on one by one until the whole sky was dotted with pinpricks of light. But no moon appeared. The fire crackled on. Zoe and her mother helped Ely and Vincent collect wood.

'Pine cones are good for burning,' Ely said. 'And the smaller branches we can break up. Make sure you knock all the snow off and stack them near to the fire to dry them.'

They busied themselves until they had a big stack of sticks and bigger branches which had fallen off the trees. Vincent had even managed to pull out a tree. No one was sure how he had done it.

They sat down in front of the fire and divided up the rest of the bread and biscuits. They gobbled it up. Her mother saved four chocolate biscuits for breakfast. Everything else was gone. Her mother sat, cross-legged and Zoe and Vincent lay down either side of her, using her legs as cushions. Zoe soon felt her eyes closing as she listened to the crackling of flames and felt the warmth from the fire.

'Zoe, Vincent, look!'

147

Zoe opened her eyes, confused for a minute as to where she was, or how long she'd been asleep for.

'What?' The fire was still crackling in front of her.

'Look!' Her mother pointed to the sky.

A band of green light crept across the sky like a giant snake digesting its weekly dinner.

'Wow, what is it?'

'It's the Northern Lights.'

Zoe closed her eyes again. The next thing she heard was the thwack-thwack-thwack of a helicopter.

Chapter 28 – The Helicopter and the Snowmobile

'Wake up! They've come to get us!'

Zoe lifted a heavy eyelid. Ely was jumping up and down near the fire. Zoe blinked. The helicopter came closer; a huge search lamp scoured the land below. Her mother held her tightly, whispering that it was going to be okay.

'They've seen us!' said Ely.

The helicopter shot snow into the air as it touched the ground. A man jumped out and came running towards them. 'Ely!' he cried. 'And you are all here!' Ely started talking in Icelandic. Two more people came out of the helicopter with blankets. Zoe felt herself being enveloped by a big blanket and taken towards the helicopter. Her mother and Vincent were behind her.

'We take you to hotel,' said Eric.

It appeared there wasn't enough room in the helicopter so, after some discussion, two of the rescuers stayed behind.

'They will come straight back to get them,' Ely explained.

They were all offered some warm chocolate from a thermos. It was the nicest thing Zoe had ever tasted. The motor switched on and the blades started turning. THWACK-THWACK-THWACK, the helicopter jumped into the green snake in the sky. Zoe watched through a small window the snake morph into witches' fingers stroking the velvet night. Down below the whiteness of the land shone the way. Zoe rested her head onto her mother's shoulder as they were whisked through the fingers in the noisy helicopter.

They landed in a school playing field and, from there, they were taken in a car to a hotel. People fussed around them but Lizzie kept saying that they were fine, they just needed to sleep. They were shown to a room with two large beds and there they fell into a deep sleep.

Zoe woke up the next morning to hear her mother talking to someone – and sighing deeply. The curtains were still drawn but light peeped over the top and around the sides.

'Mummy?' Zoe called. Vincent was still asleep next to her.

'Yes, darling,' her mother said, closing her phone. 'That was Ely. She wanted to know if we were all right.' She went over to the window and opened the curtains. Sunlight poured in.

Zoe blinked. 'Is there any news of Merida?'

'No.'

'Have they caught Balli?'

'No. They found his snowmobile in the mountains about ten kilometres east of where we were but there was no sign of Balli.'

'But how did Balli's snowmobile get there?' Zoe wondered.

'Maybe he left the engine on and let it go.'

'Oh. I hope Balli doesn't hurt Merida.'

'Merida can look after herself. Ely said they've sent out a search party to look for them. The weather is good.'

'But they will never find him if he's in Merida.'

'It's possible.'

'He might have flown back to the Faroe Islands,' Vincent said, sitting up suddenly.

Her mother sighed. 'Morning, Vincent. Let's hope not. Anyway we have a buffet breakfast to enjoy! And Ely is going to join us.'

'What's a buffet?' Vincent asked.

A buffet was a massive breakfast of cereal, yoghurts, honey, toast, chocolate spread, strawberry jam, fried egg and scrambled egg, cheese, ham, sausages, tomatoes, olives, meats, cakes, fruit salad, orange juice, apple juice. They sat down and ate everything. Ely joined them. Her long hair was shining again. But no one had found anything yet.

'At least you're safe,' Lizzie said.

'Yes, thanks to you.'

'And Merida,' Vincent said.

'And Merida.'

When they couldn't eat even a little cake more, they put on their coats and boots and went outside. They were near the slide mountain.

'There's the slide,' said Vincent, pointing. 'Let's go on it! If we do it again, I bet Balli comes to tell us off! Then we catch him. Bash!'

Ely stopped. 'You know, Vincent. That is an excellent idea.'

Zoe wasn't sure. She remembered the way Balli had twisted her mother's arm but, before she could protest, Ely started calling people and before long a large crowd had gathered on the square in front of the mountain. Eric arrived in the Cat with a pile of plastic sleds in the trailer.

'Come on, Mummy. Please come. Let's stay together.'

'Okay,' her mother said, squeezing her arm. Zoe felt a warmth seep through her.

A discussion took place amongst the people.

'They are deciding who goes and who stays,' said Ely.

In the end they decided that, at least, thirty would stay, leaving about twenty adults and children who scrambled to get into the trailer with their sleds. Eric helped them all. They chugged on up to the top. The mood was sombre. The adults didn't talk much but they all smiled at Zoe and Vincent and some talked to her mother. All Zoe understood was that Balli was bad. Vincent scraped the snow off the edges of the trailer and made it into a snowball. Soon all the children were throwing snowballs at each other. One hit Lizzie smack in the face. Zoe thought she was going to be cross but she simply brushed it off, smiling. They reached the top and Ely distributed the plastic sleds. Vincent jumped on and pushed himself off.

'I don't know if I can do this, Zoe,' her mother said.

Zoe helped her get in and they whizzed down next to each other, screaming happily. Zoe almost forgot about the missing Merida.

This time Balli arrived on foot. He came right into the square in front of the mountain slide. Many people were watching the action on the mountain and didn't see him coming. Zoe only saw him because they arrived at the same time as he did. She recognised his large lumpy head immediately and told her mother to slow down. They both dug their heels into the snow and stopped long before they reached the square. Everyone behind her also stopped, afraid to go any further. Vincent was in front, near the square. His back was to Balli. He was looking behind, looking for her. Oh dear. Balli was heading straight for Vincent. Where was Ely? As Zoe looked around, Ely flew past them.

'Stay there!' she ordered.

'Come on,' her mother muttered, standing up and pulling her sled. 'I can't leave Vincent.'

Zoe and her mother walked forward.

A silence fell.

Ely stopped two metres behind Vincent and picked up her sled. Balli was two metres in front of him. The crowd had gathered round.

Vincent looked around confused.

'Hello Balli,' said Vincent. 'Have you seen our campervan?'

'There,' said Balli.

Zoe followed his lumpy finger and there, sure enough, was Merida in exactly the same spot she'd been in when they had arrived.

Bee-beep! Bee-beep! Bee-beep! It came from Merida.

Zoe gasped and started clapping.

Ely and her mother cried out.

'Hooray!' said Vincent.

The other people looked confused. Balli looked around them. One of them spat at him. Someone else picked up a snowball and threw it at him. It landed in his face.

Zoe held her breath. Surely he would turn them all to stone. But Balli did nothing. Zoe saw Ely close her eyes for a split second.

Silence.

Then Balli held up his hand and said,

'Fyrirgefðu.'

There were gasps of incredulity.

'He said sorry,' muttered Ely. 'A troll never says sorry.'

'Sorry,' he rasped again, this time in English to Zoe, Lizzie and Vincent. 'Sorry I have treated you all so badly. I am especially sorry to Ely, Abela and Dana. Forgive me. You are welcome to use my mountain.'

He turned to walk away.

Everyone stood silently, shocked.

'Hey, Balli,' said Vincent, going after him. 'Come and have a go on your slide! Here, you can have my sled.'

Balli stopped. And then a strange thing happened. His face found new crevices and slipped into them. He smiled. 'You are very brave boy,' he said.

'Come on, Mummy,' said Zoe. She would also be brave. 'We go too.'

'Okay. Ely?'

'Yes.' Ely waved up to those still on the mountain and Eric beeped the Cat. Sleds and skiers started whizzing down. Eric came to get them. No one would join them and Eric wouldn't talk to Balli but he let him climb up. Balli said something to him and Eric gave a curt nod. Zoe, her mum and Vincent climbed in the trailer and sat opposite him. Ely borrowed an extra sled and put them all in. Zoe hoped Balli wouldn't change his mind and turn them into stone and roll them down the mountain. Or worse. But he smiled as Eric moved forward.

'Has Merida been talking to you?' Lizzie asked.

'Talk. Talk. Talk. Without stop. She is a very big-mouthed campervan.'

'Oh I know. She just won't shut up about not recycling the rubbish that our parents have given us.'

'But we have to recycle,' Zoe said. 'To save the planet.'

'Things yes,' Lizzie said. 'But, as human beings, it also important not to pass on violence and hatred as people can do even more damage than plastic.'

Zoe wasn't sure if she really understood but she felt the adults were feeling stronger and happier. Particularly Balli. He was no longer a troll.

'I'm a troll,' said Balli. 'But from now on I try to be a better one.'

Zoe reddened. Had he heard her thoughts?

'So, can we build a ski lift up your mountain?' Ely asked.

Balli replied in Icelandic.

'What did he say?' Zoe asked.

'He said he'd already spoken to Abela this morning. He's agreed for one to be built and he is even going to pay for it.'

Balli nodded.

'Wow!' said Vincent.

'Fantastic!' said Zoe.

'That is very kind, Balli.'

Once at the top, Ely, Lizzie, Zoe, Vincent and Balli lined up.

'On your marks, get set...' Vincent set off. 'Go!' Then Balli. Then Zoe, her mum and, finally, Ely. Somehow Balli thundered down past Vincent. Zoe felt the air rush by her, the sun on her face. She felt as if she were flying. This was the best thing ever. She wished she could stay here forever. They all arrived in a domino line behind Balli.

More people had gathered in the square in front of the piste. People started shouting at Balli. Ely ran up and spoke to the crowd. 'He has apologised and agreed to a ski lift everyone.' An argument broke out in Icelandic. A police van arrived and four police officers got out.

'What is happening?' Lizzie asked.

'He should be arrested!' said the man who had spat at him. 'He holds Abela and Dana as prisoners for almost a year and he causes terror for us!'

Zoe took a step back. In their black helmets and padded jackets they looked scarier than Balli. One of them unclipped some handcuffs. Everyone started talking at once. Zoe could tell that Ely was defending Balli to the main police officer and to the man who had spat. More and more people gathered. Zoe hoped that Balli didn't turn them all into stone. That would be a hard end.

Chapter 29 – Abela, Dana and a Gift

'Please,' said someone quietly in English.

It was Abela. Everyone fell silent as Abela and Dana entered the group. Balli looked down to the ground. Abela turned and talked to the police officer. He shook his head. Abela leant forward and kissed Balli on the cheek, her long blonde hair touching him like a ray of sunshine. Dana did the same. Ely smiled. The police officer said something and went to clip the handcuffs on Balli. A black hole appeared in the middle of Balli's face as he opened his mouth. Everyone covered their ears waiting for the scream but nothing came out, not even a squeak. He closed his mouth. His dark eyes fell to the floor as he let out a deep sigh.

'Please let him go,' said Vincent. 'He will go with you, won't you Balli?'

Balli nodded. The police officer looked at Vincent in surprise. Abela said something in Icelandic. He put his handcuffs away and two officers took either side of Balli's arm and led him to the police van.

'Thank you for the slide!' Vincent shouted after Balli.

'Yes, thank you!' Zoe called. 'It's the fastest slide in the world!'

Balli stopped and looked back at them.

'Come back one day,' he said.

'Yes please,' said Vincent. 'Bye.'

'Goodbye!' called Lizzie and Zoe.

He lifted his hand up to half wave and then turned back and walked towards the police van.

'Where are they taking him?' Zoe asked Ely. 'It doesn't seem fair.'

'They will take him for questioning,' explained Ely. 'He did kidnap two people remember. And he's spent the best part of his life terrorising people. He has to take responsibility. But Abela and Dana will not press charges, which means he will soon be released. Don't worry. It is amazing. I could never imagine that someone could change so much. I can't believe Merida did this.'

A bee-beep-BEEP came from the village.

'We've forgotten Merida!' said Zoe.

BEEP!

'Yes,' said Lizzie. 'It's time to go. You two have to get back to school. We're already a day late and I don't want to get into too much trouble. I've told Vincent's mum that we're having such a good time that we decided to stay a bit longer but we must get back by tomorrow at the latest.'

'Does she know we're in Iceland?' Vincent asked.

'Not exactly. I just told her we're at the fastest slide in the world. We can tell her when we're safely home. She is missing you so much. But we'll have to comb your hair before she sees you else she'll never let you go out with us again.'

Vincent didn't reply but Zoe thought that he lifted his sled up just a little more quickly than usual.

'Come on,' he said, moving his curls away from his eyes. 'Race you to Merida!'

Ely, Abela and Dana ran with them back to the campervan.

They all jumped in.

'Merida!' said Zoe. 'We missed you so much.'

'Ah, I missed you too. But you did well, Zoe, Vincent and Lizzie. I knew you'd be all right.'

'What do you mean?' Zoe asked.

'Well, I knew I could leave you.'

'You left us?' Lizzie exclaimed.

'Yes, of course. I needed to talk to Balli. I could see he was in a spot of bother as the police had nearly caught him so I rescued him.'

'But I thought he stole you?'

'No. I stole him.'

'You left us on the mountain, on our own at night in the freezing cold?' Lizzie sounded incredulous.

'Yes, I had to. But I knew you'd be okay and I knew you'd taken some food with you.'

'But I didn't think you could drive on your own.'

'Well I can when I'm in 'ME' mode. You left me in 'ME' mode, Lizzie.'

Everyone fell silent. Zoe remembered scraping 'HELP' in the snow and telling her mother about hiding Lilly's shoes. If they hadn't been left on a freezing mountain she would probably never have done that.

'Well, we survived and you did a good job, Merida,' said Ely. 'I can't believe how much he changed. All the anger just drained out of him.'

'Of course,' said Merida. 'Once we know the truth there is no need to be angry. What's the point?'

'Amazing. Thank you, Merida,' echoed Abela and Dana. 'Now, we can live in peace.'

'He may well forget and lose it again. You humans have difficulty in reprogramming yourselves. But, hopefully, not for a few days.' Merida chuckled. 'Now can we get going? I'm fed up of this cold.'

'Really? You feel heat and cold?' said Ely in amazement.

'Of course I'm cold. It's -4.'

Vincent laughed. Zoe shook her head. She wasn't cold.

'Zoe, here you are,' Abela said, handing a small sealed bag. 'They are what you asked for. They are wrapped so don't open them. Give them straight to her.'

Zoe took the bag, thanking Abela and Dana.

'Let me see!' said Vincent, poking his dark curly hair in. 'What are they for?'

Zoe took a deep breath and told him about hiding Lilly's shoes.

'I know that. I saw you.'

'Well, I asked Abela to make some new shoes. I will go back to the park to try to find Lilly.'

'Okay,' said Vincent. 'But I want to see my mummy first.'

'Yes,' said Lizzie. 'We're going. We'll get some diesel and then head off to the Faroe Islands and then back to the UK.'

'Come and visit again one day,' Ely said. 'Oh and Vincent, here's your jumper.'

'You keep it.'

'Thank you,' said Ely. 'You are a generous boy.'

Ely, Abela and Dana waved goodbye as they drove off.

Zoe sat quietly. She felt sad to be leaving. Vincent was also silent. Her mother stopped at a petrol station to fill up and bought them some more sandwiches and Kit Kats. Then they found a quiet spot and disappeared into the thin pinkish air, flying over the white tipped craggy mountains and out over the sea. As the sun sank into the water, the sky burned before settling into a dark hazy purple.

Chapter 30 – The Purple Slide

Zoe was woken up by her mother picking her up. Someone else was in the van. It was Vincent's mother. She held Vincent tightly, stroking his hair. 'You've been where, Lizzie?' she asked her mother.

'Iceland,' said her mother. 'We'll explain everything tomorrow. For now let's put them to bed. And then me. I am exhausted.'

'I bet! Iceland must have been very busy. What did you go there for? At this time of night? And, Vincent, what's happened to your hair! It's full of knots.'

'Not the shop, Mummy. Leave my hair please.'

'Hm,' said Lizzie. 'We'll explain tomorrow.'

Tomorrow dawned and Zoe woke up in her own bed next to Milly Monkey and Chipeto the donkey and her red blanket feeling good, very good. 'Sorry, you didn't get to go on the slide, Chipeto. Next time, I promise.' She hugged them both, then quickly got dressed. She couldn't wait to go to the park. But first she had to go to school. She put the bag of shoes in her rucksack so they could go on the way back.

Her mother was downstairs sorting out some tins from the camper.

'I'm afraid we have to say goodbye to Merida,' her mother said as she ate her cornflakes.

'What?' Zoe felt a sharp pain in her tummy.

'She has to go. You remember what the mechanic in the garage said. She has another family to go to.'

'But I thought she could stay a bit longer,' Zoe said.

'No, darling. There are so many people who would like to have adventures. But go and have a word with her.'

Zoe went outside into the cold flat grey Norwich day. Merida was parked in the drive. She stepped inside. Her mother had already cleaned the van and taken their things out.

'Hello Zoe,' Merida said.

'Hello Merida. Mummy says you are going?'

'Yes, I'm afraid so,' said Merida. 'There are other children who need me. Or, should I say, their parents. But we will meet up again one day, Zoe. I have given your mother a tracking app on her phone so if ever you really need me you can find me. But I don't think you will. Your mother is a star. And so are you and Vincent. Just don't ever forget that.'

'Merida, please don't go!' cried Vincent jumping into the van. 'Please! You never talked to my mummy.'

'I think your mother understands, Vincent. Your father loves you, too, but it sounds like he needs some time. Just keep well and happy, Vincent. Ah, I think you have some visitors.'

Lilly and her mother appeared at the door. Zoe's heart jumped. She hadn't expected that.

'Hello Merida, hello Zoe and Vincent. Do you remember us? We met in the park.'

'Ah! Hello Claudia and Lilly,' boomed Merida. 'Nice to hear you again.'

Zoe looked at the tall blond-haired girl and smiled. Lilly grinned back. Zoe glanced at her shoes. She was wearing off-white trainers. Zoe took a deep breath.

'I have something to tell you,' she said.

Just then her mother arrived with her school rucksack.

'Hello there,' Lizzie greeted the others. 'Fantastic to see you! We have had such an adventure.'

'We thought you would,' Claudia said, hugging Lizzie. 'We saw on our app that Merida was back so we came to see how you got on. We're just about to move to Leicester.'

'Leicester?' Lizzie sounded surprised.

Lester? Zoe suspected that would be another silly spelling.

'Well, I've just got a job there and we've rented a flat. It's not great but we will see how it goes. I start next week. Before we lived in Cromer. We love the sea.'

'Oh dear, not much sea in Leicester. Would you like a coffee? The kids should be going to school but we need to take Merida somewhere.'

'Yippee!' screamed Zoe.

'Sh! What shall we do, Merida? Back to the mechanic or perhaps to York to see that policeman?'

'I'm not sure the policeman is quite ready. I think I should go to an airport or a campervan hire place. Maybe someone will want to drive south. I don't really want to spend the summer in England or Iceland. But Zoe and Vincent can choose the next child or children.'

'What about Sheena? She's the girl who bullies me at school.'

'Someone bullies you at school?' her mother asked sharply, her green eyes piercing her.

'Of course.'

'Why have you never said?'

Zoe shrugged and turned her eyes away. She had said. But her mother hadn't believed her. Zoe hadn't mentioned it again. She had thought it was because she was different. Because she didn't have a father.

'What does she do?'

'Oh. Pulls my hair, sticks chewing gum in it, spits, calls me names.'

Everyone was silent for a moment. Then her mum came and gave her a big hug. Zoe felt warm again inside. Her mother was on her way to earning a skyful of stars, even if she did still sometimes look at Facebook and no doubt she would continue to work, tidy-up, cook, lie-down, shop, have a glass of wine with Annie. But now, Zoe knew, it would be different.

'You know let us work this one out,' her mother said. 'While it would be good to change Sheena, I think we also have to learn how to deal with these people.'

'Okay,' said Zoe. 'I think I can handle her now.'

'Well said, Zoe,' said Merida.

Lizzie gave Zoe an extra big hug and kissed her head. 'There are a few campervan hire places in Norfolk but I doubt anyone will want to go south,' said Lizzie.

'How about an airport?' suggested Vincent.

'Good idea, Vincent. Let me look on my phone.' Lizzie let go of Zoe and thumbed her phone.

'How about Heathrow airport? There's a campervan rental that hires campervans out and suggests trips to France and Austria.'

'Austria! In November. No, thank you,' said Merida. 'But maybe I can persuade them to go to Spain.'

'Then we drive to Heathrow and get the bus back. It's about a four hour journey. Maybe we can fly? Merida?'

'Okay, just this once.'

Zoe and Vincent clapped in excitement.

'What about the documents? How do we get them changed over so quickly?' asked Lizzie.

'There's someone called Dan at the campervan rental. He'll deal with it,' said Merida.

'How do you know?'

Merida chuckled.

'And can my mummy come this time?' asked Vincent.

'Yes, I will go and ask her.'

'We have to get going but may I just have a little chat with Merida?' asked Claudia.

'Yes, of course. I'll go and make the coffee. Do you want to show Lilly your bedroom?' Lizzie asked Zoe.

Vincent found a football in the front garden and started kicking it. Zoe took Lilly by the hand and led her upstairs.

'I have that!' Lilly said, picking up one of her Playmobil horses.

'Here you are.' Zoe gave her the bag with the shoes in.

'What is it?' Lilly asked.

'I'm sorry, Lilly,' Zoe began, 'but it was me. I hid your shoes in the park that day.'

Lilly didn't say anything but shrugged dismissively.

'I have got you some new ones.'

Lilly opened the bag and pulled out a pair of beautiful yellow shoes with a silver buckle over the front. Zoe wondered how Abela had known Lilly's shoes were yellow. They were the best.

'Wow! Thank you! Here, that's not all. There's more. This pair must be for you!' Lilly pulled out another pair of shoes. The same except purple. She gave the pair to Zoe.

Zoe gasped. The soft shoes fitted like a glove. Lilly did the same.

'They are perfect!' Lilly said.

Then a strange thing happened. As Zoe stood up and walked around the room she felt as if she was bouncing.

'Magic shoes!' Zoe cried.

'Wow! Who made them?' Lilly said, spinning round.

'The elves,' Zoe said. 'We were in Iceland, you know.'

'Amazing. Look in the bag again. There are more.'

Zoe looked in and pulled out a small pair of silver and black trainers with the same silver buckle. 'For Vincent!'

Zoe and Lilly bounced down the stairs to show the adults and to give the pair to Vincent. They all admired the shoes. Vincent put his on and began leaping around. The ball almost seemed to dance around the shoes. He looked like a professional footballer.

After gulping down chocolate milk, they all bounced to the park. Even the adults had a spring in their step. Her mother didn't complain about the grey cardboard shoeboxes as she always did and Zoe skipped over the Walkers crisp bags and pizza box on the pavement. She just knew that, this time, she would fly down the slide. A smile stretched across her face and she felt her chest quiver with excitement. She just knew she would never hurt anyone again. It didn't make her feel good. This was how it felt to feel good. She wanted to feel like this forever. She didn't care if the big boys were there. Or Sheena. They couldn't touch her now. And if they did, it didn't matter. She would always have herself. And her mum. And Vincent. And Lilly. And Merida would never be far away.

She flew down the slide behind Lilly. As she looked behind it glimmered PURPLE. Zoe laughed and bounced back up the steps, her feet hardly touching the ground.